I0603313

FIVE DRAGONS

A DRAGONS OF ERIDAN COLLECTION

PAMELA JEFFS

Formatting and cover design by Four Ink Press
Edited by Rare Bird Editing
Interior artwork by Sara Williams
Language: Australian English

ISBN:
978-0-6481442-5-0 (pbk)
978-0-6481442-6-7 (e-bk)

Visit www.fourinkpress.com

To Darren.
For always being proud of my achievements.
Thank you.

REVIEWS

Jeffs' beautifully-wrought language slides you effortlessly into the strangest of worlds. Another poignant, fascinating collection.

Aiki Flinthart, author of the Kalima Chronicles

Five Dragons is a highly imaginative, genre-bending collection of interlinked stories whose entirety achieves an ambitious goal. A true personification of a story cycle where texts are held together by collective protagonists, recurring characters and the dominant motif herein of dragons in an ancient war that blasts into the future, the compilation is so well done it reads like a novel.

Eugen Bacon, author of Claiming T-Mo and Writing Speculative Fiction

CONTENTS

INTRODUCTION

Here live dragons.
All kinds.
And their stories are connected.
Welcome to the world of Eridan.

Amberwing:

Stolen Futures

Adeen, bringing breakfast for her dragon, pauses. Across the courtyard, the huge door to the hatchery hangs damaged, its planks splintered and iron bandings buckled. The bucket of chicken carcasses she holds drops from her fingers. It clatters loudly to the ground, spilling dead birds out across the flagstones. Adeen sprints for the door, her heart pounding. The Amberwing hatchery has been breached.

Inside, voices collide against each other, echoing within the cavernous nesting chamber. The dragon mothers huddle on stone nests, copper wings fanned out protectively over their eggs. Adeen slows, listening to the angry murmurs.

'How dare a human steal from us!'

'The Accords should be revoked. Let us fly. Blood for blood.'

'But our eggs. We cannot leave them.'

The largest dragon, Ketu, speaks over the others. 'Settle yourself, sisters. The Accords shall not be broken until we know more. We must hunt the perpetrator down, seek answers, and deliver justice appropriately.'

Adeen calls out, her voice small amid the dragons, 'Queen Ketu, what has transpired here?'

Ketu's glowing, black-opal eyes flare as they fall on Adeen. 'Treachery has transpired! We returned from our hunt to find one of our nests attacked. Your job is to protect our eggs while we are away. Where were you?'

A nest attacked? Adeen reels. *But the hatchery is in the centre of the village, well lit and protected. How could that happen?*

Ketu raises her head. She bares the length of her teeth and huffs, sending a carrion-laced breath rolling past. 'Your silence rightfully attests your shame. Now go and make yourself useful. Attend your queen, Keeper,' says Ketu. 'Rahu has need of you.'

Rahu? Rahu's eggs have been attacked? Adeen, shocked, turns towards her dragon. Rahu, the smallest of the Amberwing mothers currently nesting, keens over her empty nest; the same one Adeen tended last night as the dragon mothers, including Rahu, had hunted.

She left early. The eggs were safe and warm, the hatchery quiet. There was no need to stay…

But Rahu's clutch is now missing except for a single egg—an egg that lies shattered in the bottom of her cart-sized nest.

Adeen kneels at Rahu's side. Amongst the fragments of shell lies the still corpse of a baby dragon. Even in death, his scales shine like his mother's, a mix of gold and copper. His tiny eyes are closed—never having opened to see life.

Adeen feels sick. Such a crime. Amberwing dragons raise only one clutch of eggs in their long lifetimes. The loss of even one egg is a tragedy. Rahu, still keening, leans down and gently lifts the dead baby in her mouth. Adeen looks away as the mother dragon consumes the tiny body.

Such is the manner of dragons.

But with one lost, there are still two eggs missing. And until they are found, the Peace Accords, so fragile between dragon and human, hang in the balance.

Adeen dares not think what will happen if the treaty is sundered. The dragons, if roused, could decimate humanity.

For the moment the Accords, by Ketu's command, still stand. Adeen turns away from thoughts of politics and gives her full attention to her dragon. She dares to offer comfort by placing a hand on Rahu's muscular foreleg. The heat of the mother's rage and grief radiates out of her skin.

'Rahu,' says Adeen. 'I have failed you, my Queen.'

Rahu's nostrils flare, glowing with the brightness of her luminous, acid breath. 'This is not your doing, Adeen,' she growls. 'This is the work of a mage.'

A mage? Adeen looks back into the nest at the broken eggshell, all that remains of a tiny dragon's lost life. Yes, a mage could be the answer. They steal and ingest the eggs to heighten their magic. 'Perhaps, my Queen. A mage would have reason. But which one would dare such a thing?'

Rahu's eyes, akin to her sister Ketu's, swirl, two whirlpools of colour and darkness. 'The hatchery records list the names of all known mages. Go. Make a list of those that dwell closest. We will travel to see them. Even if those are innocent, they may have answers for us. With two of my eggs still missing, we need to try everything.'

***

The hatchery library holds the collected history of the world of Eridan. Lines of books weigh down the ancient shelves like anvils. Adeen huddles over a table, a thick tome open before her. In the puddle of lamplight, her finger traces a list inked onto the cream parchment—all the mages known to exist in the country.

Many of the names are crossed through with thick lines; those belonging to the magic weavers killed in the Accord War. The ones that remain and their last known locations are listed in the neat writing of the librarian. Adeen's finger pauses next to one, halfway down the list.

The only mage dwelling in these lands.

And it doesn't bode well.

He is a war criminal.

Adeen leans over the clean sheet of parchment next to her. Her quill scratches across the surface, inking in the details.

- Black John / The Ruined Moorlands

The library door creaks open. Adeen quickly closes the book and folds the parchment in half. A slim shadow steals past the shelves just out of the lamplight, but a familiar voice addresses her.

'Well met, Adeen.'

Jonah, her friend, is the dragon Ketu's keeper. He's still dressed in his work clothes, the leather vest marred by dragon acid and chicken blood. He steps into the circle of lamplight, his shoulder-length brown hair glinting like caramel. He is the same age as Adeen, seventeen, and handsome in his own way with his smooth, dark skin and pale, almost white, eyes. But here in the darkened library, the shifting light is unkind to him. Shadows play across the planes of his face, making him look ghoulish.

'Jonah,' she says. 'How fare you this evening?'

The boy is unusually solemn with his eyes downcast and brow furrowed. 'I heard what happened,' he says. His knuckles look like polished oak as he pulls out the chair next to Adeen. The legs scrape quietly across the flagstone floor. He sits.

Adeen looks back to the book on the table. Her fingertip follows the intricate lines of the flower patterns pressed into the leather cover. 'Yes.'

'You will go with Rahu?'

'Of course.'

'Would you remain here if I asked you to?'

Adeen smiles. Jonah has always sought to protect her, ever since they were children—ever since she arrived, an orphan, to Hatchery Town. 'You would go if it were Ketu.'

Jonah rubs his shoulder. 'I am certain I would not be given the chance. If I ever failed Ketu, she would kill me.'

'Our dragons are exacting, Jonah, but they do love us. In their own way.'

Jonah smiles, but the warmth of it does not reach his eyes. 'Yes. They are exacting.'

Adeen shrugs to lighten the mood. She swings the book across the table to face Jonah and opens it. Jonah's forehead crinkles as he leans over to read the list of names.

'You think a mage is the thief?'

'Rahu thinks so and I agree,' replies Adeen. 'Who else would benefit from stealing Amberwing eggs?'

'It is a good place to begin.' He taps a finger on the name that Adeen has already chosen. 'Black John. We should start with him.'

'We?'

'I will journey with you.'

'By Ketu's command?'

'By command of my heart.' Jonah's eyes glitter as they lift and catch Adeen's. 'I wish you returned home safely.'

Adeen chuckles. 'I will welcome the company,' she says, genuinely glad his familiar strength will be there to support her on the quest to come.

***

The air rushing past Adeen's ears is cold enough to freeze. Having prepared through the night, Rahu, Jonah and she are finally headed for the Ruined Moorlands. Adeen huddles lower on Rahu's back, listening to her steady wing beats and the creak of the leather saddle straps. She is grateful for the point of warmth against her back where Jonah sits with his arms around her. Over to the left, the dawn sun crests the mountains. The rays catch the copper edges of Rahu's wings, making them gleam. Adeen pulls her shoulders in closer and smiles. In contrast to the mountains, still cloaked in indigo shadow, her Rahu is a jewel of the skies.

Adeen's thoughts turn to the Ruined Moorlands and the mage who lives there. Black John. She's not looking forward to the confrontation. Rumour has it the mage was the deadliest in the Accord Wars. Slaughtering human and dragon alike, he earned the reputation of a vicious killer—and worse, she found in the hatchery files, he was accused of drinking dragon blood to strengthen his magic.

Adeen wonders at the accuracy of such tales. Dragon blood is caustic; surely a man, even heightened to the skills of a mage, would perish if he consumed it? Besides, it was the magic in dragon blood, the blood of the great drake Sheerwing, that defeated the mage and bound him. If blood strengthened Black John, how would it have the power to bind him?

Rahu's muscles bunch under Adeen's thighs as the dragon dips into a dive. Adeen grips Rahu's neck to hold her seat, and the pressure of Jonah's hands around her waist tightens. From under Rahu's extended wing, the deep valley they seek emerges with its steep sides and hollow, sodden bowl. The Ruined Moorlands, still shrouded in pre-dawn shadows.

From this high, the lay of the black and grey landscape is clear. Cracked rocks, deep bogs and broken forests line the length of the crevasse. The spindly limbs of long-drowned trees reach skyward, fingers like skeletons, a frozen reminder of darker times when this land was ruled by war and life held less meaning.

Deep in the shadow under the fall of a mighty cliff rises a low hill of rugged stone. From here, Sheerwing's immense skeleton can be seen encasing the mound. His petrified bones, stained black and green with moss and poisoned lichen, are Black John's prison.

Rahu lands awkwardly on the uneven ground. Her claws find purchase on rough stone, but her tail catches the edge of a black puddle. The liquid slews sideways into the air. Adeen holds her sleeve to her nose. The disturbed water smells of sickly rot and death.

Jonah's nose wrinkles at the rising stench. 'Where to from here?' he asks.

Rahu sidles to the left, lifting her tail clear of the black slop. 'Filthy moors,' she snarls, flicking the putrid liquid from her scales. She looks up towards the hill. 'We search for Sheerwing's skull. The mouth of the drake is the doorway to Black John's prison.'

Adeen loosens the saddle belts and slides to the ground. Jonah follows. 'Lead the way, Queen,' says Adeen. 'We follow.'

Rahu shakes her wings. Their lengths of draping skin and scales clatter like sails in the wind as she shuffles them into place along her sides. Then she lifts her long neck into the sky, arching its graceful length like a swan's. The spines that encircle it rise to full extension. Their sensitive tips quiver as Rahu scents the air. For a moment there is nothing but the hum of stinging insects waking in the moor. Rahu settles her spines and looks down at Adeen and Jonah.

'This way.' She turns to lead the humans deeper into the moorlands.

The rugged terrain hinders quick progress. Boots sink one moment into bog, and then slip on wet, slime-covered stone the next. Adeen is thankful for her thick riding leathers, their sturdy construction protecting her at least from the stinging nettles and insects. Jonah walks just ahead of her. As he moves silently through the dead trees, Adeen takes in the details of him—his familiar outline, the way his hair is pulled back and curls at the nape of his neck. But even out in the air, he looks sickly. Adeen wonders if her friend is ill, wonders if she should have asked him to stay home, but knows he would have refused.

Ahead, Rahu stops. Ten more paces and Adeen reaches her side. All thoughts of Jonah flee.

Just ahead rests Sheerwing.

The great drake's skull lies half tilted on a mound of flaked stone. The bone is black, but the eye sockets seem to glow as if they still harbour a vestige of life. Long rows of silver teeth hang from the jawbones, their sharp tips points of light in the dank, dead landscape. And they are full of magic; their brightness attests to that. This is the entry to Black John's prison. To get to him, they must pass through those jaws and hope the teeth take no offence to their intrusion. Already the bloodied bones of some animal lie jumbled below Sheerwing's mouth. They do not make Adeen feel any better. Their existence tells the story—that those teeth can and will snap shut on you.

Rahu's chuckle is warm. 'Do not look so fearful, Adeen,' she says. 'Sheerwing may be earthbound, his soul tied to his bones, but he must still eat. The ingested souls maintain his magic and keep the world safe from Black John.' She swings her chin towards the carcass. 'And those remains attest that he has already feasted this day. We are safe to pass.'

But Adeen doesn't feel so sure.

The light dims and the atmosphere cools as Adeen enters Sheerwing's skull. She hunches her shoulders, following Rahu. The darkness deepens further, pressing down on Adeen's head. She worries about the weight in the petrified bone arching over her, and the enormity of the dragon's presence trapped within it.

Curtains of moss grow in the darkest parts. They hang from the ceiling, the damp fingers of vegetation brushing against Adeen's arms and cheeks. The plants feel slimy, like the touch of damp seaweed. Adeen tries to focus her fear. She begins to count her steps. One step becomes twenty, then becomes one hundred.

Finally, a glow appears ahead, and Rahu's silhouette sharpens against the luminescence. Adeen's spirits lift.

The light comes from a hole in the back of Sheerwing's skull. But it's no ordinary radiance. It is a portal, multicoloured and shimmering—a dragon-forged doorway leading to the alternate dimension where Black John is held captive.

Again, Rahu leads the way, scrabbling down the roughened bone. She steps into the light and disappears, the surface of the gateway left rippling in her wake. A wash of electricity trickles over Adeen's shoulders as she passes next. She recognises the touch of a complex imprisonment spell threaded through the portal's magic—a ward built and sustained by Sheerwing and one, she realises when she emerges, that protects a startling garden glade.

The beauty of the new dimension comes as a shock after the misery of the moorlands. Here, protected by Sheerwing's magic, life thrives under a clear, pale violet sky. There is no sense of containment, only a scene painted in butterflies, flowers and fine green grass. Further along, a line of old weeping willows marks the edge of a sparkling stream, the water in it dancing like diamonds in the light.

The rattle of rocks draws Adeen's attention away. Jonah, climbing out of the dragon's skull, has stumbled on his last step. He falls flat to the ground and moans.

Adeen rushes to his side. 'Are you all right?'

He doesn't answer. Adeen places a hand on his brow, meeting fevered skin. His face is grey and the white of his eyes, yellow.

'I thought we would never be free of that place,' whispers Jonah.

'What ails you, Keeper Jonah?' Rahu's voice is firm, but not unkind.

Adeen turns to the dragon. 'He is ill, Queen. I fear he can go no further.'

Rahu drops her nose and snuffs at Jonah's shirt. The colours in her eyes swirl as she breathes in his scent deeper. 'Yes,' she whispers. 'There is a strange sickness about him, one I do not recognise.' Her voice grows louder. 'But we cannot linger here for him. We must find the mage.'

'I will not abandon him, Queen,' says Adeen. 'He came of his own accord to help us. We should attend to him.'

Rahu's head lifts sharply, her offence at Adeen's words palpable. The claws on her front feet—ten long, ebony scythes—extend and dig into the ground. The smell of torn earth rises. 'Are you suggesting a human is of more value than my eggs,' says the dragon, her voice low and dangerous.

'Not to you, fierce Queen,' replies Adeen. 'But consider this. My friendship to him means the same to me as your eggs mean to you. Please do not ask me to leave him. He is my friend.'

Rahu considers Adeen for a moment. The swirl in her eyes slows. The fire leaves her voice. 'Your loyalty to him is admirable,' says the dragon. 'And so I will defer, but only to a point. You are my keeper and must attend me. So, make Jonah comfortable. We will continue on together and if we can, we will return for him.'

If we can. Adeen's heart sinks. *What am I thinking? We go to fight a mage! We may well not return.*

Adeen holds her thoughts to herself; she does not want Rahu to see her fear. She bows her head. 'Thank you, Queen.'

'Make haste with your preparations.' The dragon glances over her shoulder. 'My eggs are waiting.'

***

With Jonah settled by the stream, Adeen follows Rahu. She clings close to the dragon's side as they move deeper into the glade. Past shrubs of unearthly flowers and bright-winged birds flitting amongst the trees, Adeen finds the beauty of the place almost hypnotising.

'Why is it so beautiful here, Queen, if it is intended to be a prison?'

Rahu keeps walking, her reptilian feet swishing through tussocks of sweet grass. 'A dragon's magic is reflective of its nature,' she says. 'Sheerwing was a Glamourwing, a dragon obsessed with beauty. When he sacrificed himself to save the world, his heart maintained its passion, and so his magic reflects that.'

'It hardly seems fair,' replies Adeen, 'that a criminal is allowed to live in such a place.'

Rahu shrugs a scaled shoulder. 'Immortal mages are dark creatures. Beauty terrifies them. Rest assured, this place truly is a prison for Black John.'

The path by the stream ends at a bridge. Past the weeping willows, the small, stone span reaches elegantly for the opposite bank. Its white-quartz railings gleam in the sunlight, sparkling like freshly fallen snow. But not all of its construction is pristine. The far end of the bridge is marred, its clean stone charred black with burnt magic and dragon acid.

Rahu slows to a stop. Her nostrils widen as she sniffs the air. 'A battle,' she says, as if to herself. She sniffs again. 'Between mage and dragon.'

Adeen pulls a small dagger she has holstered at her side. Usually its sharp edge is used to divide up chicken carcasses for the dragons. She feels better having it in her hand. 'I'll go and look,' she says.

The heat of mage magic blisters off the stonework of the bridge. It leaches through the soles of Adeen's boots and singes her feet. She crosses quickly, past the scored stone and the blackened edges of granite.

Three steps beyond the edge of the bridge, Adeen finds the body of Black John.

The mage lies against the whorled bole of a pepper tree. His long, dreadlocked hair is white, desaturated with age, but his beard is as black as night. His skin droops, raw and peeling, from his face as if burned with acid. The blue cloak wrapped around him is ruined also, marred with scorch marks and blood, congealed. So much blood—he did not die easily or well. Adeen chokes back her horror. This is not the first dead man she has seen, but it is the first she has witnessed brutally murdered.

Adeen hears Rahu crossing the bridge. Her steps are soft, the rasp of her tail slithering like a snake over stone. 'What have you found?' asks the dragon.

'I think it is Black John.' Adeen looks over her shoulder. 'He appears to be dead.'

'Dead? Impossible!'

'Murdered. Come see for yourself, Queen.'

Rahu walks up to the body. She sniffs, then huffs the smell of the mage's blood out of her nostrils. Her head begins to sway. Her jaws grind in agitation. 'But a mage cannot be killed,' she says. 'How can this have happened? To have come all this way for nothing—I need answers!'

Adeen doesn't want to look at Black John's body anymore. She turns away from the sorry sight and walks back to inspect the bridge. 'The stone,' she says. 'It's scored with dragon acid. Perhaps the answers are not to be found with the mages, but with your own kind.'

Rahu's eyes narrow. 'Are you accusing dragons of thievery? What would be the point? They have no use for my eggs.'

'I do not have the answers, Queen. I speak only of theories.'

Rahu leaves the body of Black John. She stalks up to the bridge as if it were prey. She leans into the stonework. The sunlight catches her movement and reflects the light off her scales onto the corrupted stone. Her eyes flare as she more closely inspects the marks on the bridge. Her voice is soft when she speaks. 'You are correct. These are made by Amberwing acid.'

'An Amberwing?' asks Adeen. 'Are you sure, Queen?'

'Of course I am sure!' snaps the dragon. 'Would you not know your own weapon if you saw it? This is Amberwing acid. The only thing on this planet strong enough to melt through stone.' She turns thoughtful. 'Could it be that it is also strong enough to kill a mage?'

Adeen reluctantly looks back at the body of Black John—his melted skin and ruined cloak. Death by caustic dragon acid would be a terrible way to die.

But Rahu does not care about such things. Her concern is only for herself. 'We need to return home,' she says. 'Now.'

***

Jonah is upright when they return to him. He no longer looks sick, and he is no longer alone.

Ketu, the huge Amberwing dragon, stands by his side. Her presence surprises Adeen. An Amberwing mother doesn't usually leave a clutch of eggs behind without her keeper there to watch over them.

So why is she here?

Rahu voices Adeen's question. 'What are you doing here?' Rahu saunters up to the larger dragon. Adeen wonders if Ketu notices the suspicion in Rahu's tone.

'Well met, Rahu,' replies Ketu. 'I am here to see if you have found your answers, or better yet your eggs.'

Adeen does not miss the sarcasm in Ketu's voice.

'I have found a dead mage,' replies Rahu. Her gaze swivels to fall on Jonah. 'And perhaps another human that has risen to take his place.'

Ketu smiles, a wide grin filled with ivory teeth. 'Yes. I killed Black John, and my keeper has drunk his blood. He is on his way to becoming a mage. His powers are increasing every day. He is the real reason I am here to talk with you.'

Adeen feels her stomach fall into her feet. Jonah is becoming a mage? Suddenly his pallor and sickness take on a new, more threatening aspect. She tries to catch his gaze, but he avoids it.

Ketu speaks on. 'Rahu, I would ask you to join me in a quest to return all dragons to superiority. A quest to sunder the Accords.'

'Why would I wish such a thing?' replies Rahu. 'The Accords, while not perfect, benefit both humans and dragon.'

'And what care should we have for humans?' snarls Ketu. 'They are nothing unless manipulated to become our tools.' She gestures at Jonah with her nose. 'This boy was weak and wanting. Now look at him—I have made my keeper a most formidable weapon, and he is mine to wield.'

Rahu shakes her head. 'What you have done to this boy is a crime, Ketu.'

'Not a crime. An upgrade. You should consider the same for your own keeper. The blood you need is but across the bridge.' Ketu's lip curls. 'Perhaps if you do it, the girl will not fail you again.'

'My keeper's strengths are born from her humanity!' replies Rahu. 'I will not change her.'

As the dragons speak, Adeen finally catches Jonah's eye. But he is no longer *her* Jonah. His eyes shine in a most wicked way—red sparks of light filling their depths.

'Let me put this another way, Rahu,' says Ketu. 'If you don't join me, I will have my keeper break the other eggs we took from you.'

'YOU stole them!' screams Rahu. 'You killed my son and abducted my daughters!' Rahu does not wait for an answer. She attacks with the full fury of a grieving mother. She levels a stream of acid at Ketu. The orange liquid splatters down her chin, onto the grass and across Ketu's hide. The stench of burnt grass and charred dragon skin rises.

Before Ketu can respond, Jonah steps forward to protect his queen. A blaze of red fire streams from his fingertips and encases both him and Ketu. Thwarted, Rahu screams again. She opens her wings and launches at the newly born mage.

With head and claws and teeth, Rahu tears at the mage-fire. It falls beneath her onslaught and Jonah falls with it. He is flung aside as Rahu latches on to Ketu's neck and wrestles the larger dragon to the ground.

Adeen rushes to Jonah's side. The boy is dazed, and for the moment his eyes are his own. His fist catches in Adeen's shirt. 'You have… have to end this. Kill Ketu… kill me,' he begs.

Adeen stares at him in horror. 'No. I can't. Don't ask me to do that.'

Jonah grabs Adeen's wrist. He moves her hand, the hand that still holds her blade to his chest. He presses down with the tip of the knife. 'If you wait too long, only Rahu's acid will be able to kill me.' He glances across at Ketu, then back. 'She made me watch Black John die. Please… Adeen, don't let me die like that… not like that…'

The two dragons are battling in the background. Savage roars and snarls echo out through Sheerwing's glade. Rahu is winning for the moment, her claws having taken one of Ketu's eyes.

Adeen wishes she were anywhere else but here. But she knows the hard task must fall to her. She must do as her friend asks. First though, a question needs answering. 'Where are Rahu's eggs, Jonah?'

Jonah coughs. His eyes blaze red for a second, he shakes his head, and they shift back to his own pale gaze. 'Gone—given to merfolk at Amorpha city. Ketu forced me. She's hell-bent on starting a war, and the eggs were her way to do it. I'm sorry, Adeen. It's already done. Tell Rahu also… I am sorry.'

Adeen nods, the mystery now solved. She brushes Jonah's fringe out of his eyes. 'Are you ready?' she whispers.

'Yes. Do it.'

Adeen takes a breath and leans in, pressing down on the blade. Jonah gasps. The heat of his blood on her palm matches the heat of her tears. The sounds of the battling dragons fade into the distance.

The outcome of their fight no longer matters.

Because the Accords have already been broken.

And the ancient war between dragonkind and humans has resumed.

Hydraclaw: Legacy

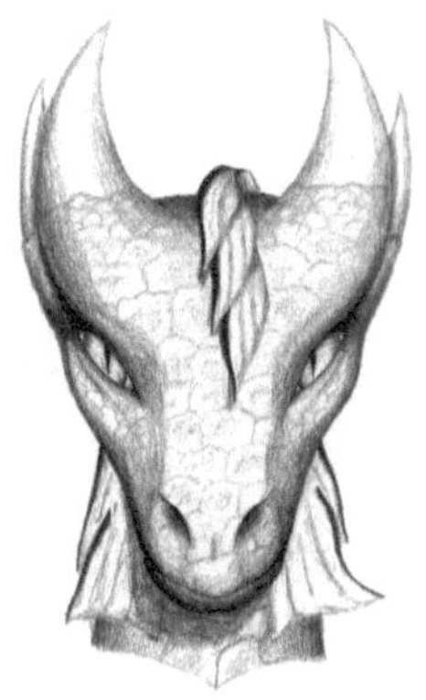

Vega, in his humanoid form, moves down the hallway like a shadow across water. His black-scaled skin seems to absorb the light from the sleek chandeliers hanging overhead. His boots click an anxious tattoo against the polished tile floor.
He has waited a long time for this day, this day and its promise of new beginnings.

The door to the meeting room slides open on his approach. Inside, Lorn is already with the blue-haired smuggler, sharing small talk and familiar smiles. A wrapped package lies between them on the wide, glass-topped table. The smuggler, dressed only in her silver-blue scales, is a merwoman from Amorpha—the ruined city that lies, half-submerged, off the rugged coast of the mainland. She has shed her tail for this meeting, choosing instead to present with the more practical shape of lengthy, human legs.

'Have you succeeded?' asks Vega, trying to sound calm.

The beautiful smuggler raises her pointed chin. She smiles, her lips peeling back to reveal sharp, needle-like teeth. 'Of course, Your Majesty. The Naia Clan does not disappoint.'

'And they are female? You are sure of it?'

The merwoman nods. 'Yes. Our midwives have confirmed it.'

'How can they be certain?' asks Vega.

'I'm told the female eggs differ in shape to the male ones.'

Vega's heart soars. He opens his claw-tipped hand and points to the package on the table. 'Please. Show us what you have acquired.'

The merwoman steps forward. With long, tapered fingers she teases away the waxed wrappings, revealing two large, bronze eggs. Their colour is a stunning contrast against the black and silver hues of Vega's meeting room.

'Two female dragon eggs, as ordered,' says the merwoman, pushing her sapphire hair back over one shoulder.

Vega looks at Lorn. 'They're perfect.'

'Indeed they are, my King.'

'Go,' says Vega. 'Prepare the lab. I will bring them there shortly.'

Lorn bows then turns to the merwoman. 'Until next time, Naunet.'

The merwoman smiles, her gaze lingering on Lorn as he leaves.

Vega wonders if there is more between them than a professional relationship. If so, it would be a strange, childless union, but not unheard of.

'The eggs,' says Vega, pulling back Naunet's attention. 'Can you tell me what breed they are?'

'Yes. Amberwing,' she says. 'Acid-spitting, sky dragons.'

'Impressive,' says Vega. 'Amberwings are decidedly uncivilised. How did you ever acquire their eggs?'

Naunet shrugs, the movement sending her hair rippling like water down her back. 'In the end it was an above-board trade. No duplicity needed. A queen dragon apparently learned of our desire to obtain eggs. She sent her representative to us and had him "donate" them to our cause. The queen's name was Ketu, I believe.'

'How strange for a queen to give up her own eggs.' Vega's brow furrows. He traces a finger down the coppery curve of the closest one. 'But we are thankful. Here in Ocerei, they will be safe, treasured above all others.' Vega's gaze returns to Naunet. 'Thank you,' he says. 'Your people have secured our future.'

Naunet places a fist on her chest. A merfolk sign of respect. 'We are ancient friends, the Naia Clan and the Hydraclaw Weyr. The Accord War took much from all of us, but most of all from your kind. We are glad to help.'

'How can I repay the Naia Clan?' asks Vega.

'There is no need, Your Majesty,' replies Naunet. 'These eggs are Empress Naia's gift to you. You granted her aid during the war. She bids you to take them with her blessing and rebuild your society.'

Vega swallows. Such an offering! He *has* lost much, and there is still so much to lose if Lorn's plan to rebuild the Hydraclaw nation fails. With all female Hydraclaw dragons slaughtered in the Accord War, their entire civilisation faces annihilation. No females means no children, means no legacy.

Means extinction.

But Hydraclaws do not give up so easily. Vega tilts his head. 'Please convey my eternal gratitude to your empress, and the hope that her gift will bear fruit.'

'I shall,' says Naunet. She pauses a moment before continuing, 'Lorn will not fail you. He is a good dragon and a talented scientist.'

'He is,' replies Vega. 'If anyone can succeed, it will be him.'

Naunet bows. 'I will take my leave, King Vega. I hope to hear glad tidings in the near future.'

***

Lorn, dressed in his white lab coat, is leaning over a microscope when Vega enters the laboratory. Next to him on the workbench lie two syringes filled with samples of dragon blood pilfered from the genetic coders. One glitters gold and the other ebony black. Amberwing and Hydraclaw. He looks up, his slitted yellow eyes gleaming. 'I think this is going to work. Take a look.' He steps back from the microscope and gestures to it. Vega hands the eggs to Lorn and bends to look into the eyepiece.

'See? The blood types are compatible,' says Lorn.

Vega watches the cells swirling on the plate beneath the scope. The different bloods, in a symphony of gold and black, meld and shift together in harmony. Sky dragon and water dragon, Amberwing and Hydraclaw, their DNA coalescing to become something more than the parts of the singular. For a moment, Vega's conscience pricks at him. Are they monsters for shifting the future of two innocent hatchlings? He steps back from the scope and glances at the two eggs cradled in Lorn's arms. On his word, their DNA will be re-coded so they will be born, no longer Amberwings, and not really Hydraclaws either, but a mix of both. Something between a fierce warrior reptile and an amphibious, morphing one.

Vega wishes it could be different. He wishes he could save his people without stealing the rightful futures of these unborn dragons.

Vega nods, ignoring the heaviness in his heart. 'Wonderful news, Lorn. Begin the process. It's time we reclaim our future.'

***

Vega doesn't feel like staying in the lab to watch Lorn work. Instead he heads for the outer platforms. He presses his palm to the pad, and the door to the sub-dive room opens. This particular room is reserved for royalty. It's been a long time since he came here, but tonight Vega feels the need to revisit old memories.

The room is as opulent as he remembers. The soft, cured-seaweed fabric lounges are still covered with their silver throws and the low, sleek abalone tables gleam. Central to the room, a wide, deep pool sparkles in the light thrown from shell-shaped wall lamps. A clever system of automated underwater hatches, built below the waterline, maintains the room pressure against the wild ocean beyond.

Vega sighs. For a moment he recalls the smell of his wife's perfume. Wild sea lily. But the memory fades in the same way the exact details of her face have faded over the years. He looks around. His last night with her was spent here; the last night before she headed off to spearhead the final battle of the Accord War and the last night before she was killed alongside her battle sisters—every female dragon of his race.

Vega refuses to dwell on his losses. Instead he takes comfort in knowing his warriors' sacrifices were not in vain. The war was settled by that battle, and the Accords came to be—the treaty that aligned dragons and humans with unity of purpose. The world created that day is the world of peace Vega will raise his new daughters in.

Vega strips off his clothes and neatly folds them, placing them on the table closest to the pool. He moves to stand at the edge of the water, letting his toes dip slightly in. He stretches out his hands, letting his claws extend. He pauses a moment, considering their polished ebony lengths. Such claws are weaponry for less developed creatures. But for a Hydraclaw, they are tools for creation. Claws like these built their great underwater city, Ocerei. They have, in the wake of the Accord War, created advanced weapon systems and discovered the keys to genetic modification and development. Vega frowns. Perhaps they are still weapons, but of a different kind.

Vega lets all thoughts of loss, technology and politics fall away. He counts to three and lets the force of the will holding his current shape fade. While a humanoid body, with its acute dexterity, is vital for the pursuit of technological advancement, there is nothing quite like existing in his true form; nothing quite like escaping the stifling atmosphere of the city domes and swimming free as nature intended.

Vega's body needs no coercing to remember its true lines. It begins to morph, his hands and feet flattening and thinning as they shift into fins. His body lengthens, surging and swelling to triple its size. Vega falls to his hands and knees. His back legs join, entwining together and thickening into a tapered cylinder of corded muscle. His face pulls forward, his cheekbones realigning and his teeth shifting. Then wings emerge from his elongated shoulders; four long, ephemeral sails, transparent and shimmering. They ripple with colours to match his other fins—luminescent blue shot through with scarlet red.

Vega, now serpentine in form, roars. He extends his wings back like a huge butterfly, dips forward, and sinks into the depths of the pool.

***

Luminous deep-sea jellyfish break the darkness of the ocean. The creatures cast their ethereal glow over the city, clouds of pale green stars hovering in the underwater sky. Vega stretches his wings and opens his senses. He relishes the feel of the salty currents reaching for him, filling his gills and catching his wings to carry him higher. The higher he goes, the more of the city comes into view.

Ocerei.

Her huge glass domes dot the ocean floor in a semi-circular pattern. Seven domes in total, but only four are illuminated. Those closest to the cliff edge, the women's quarters, stand dark and silent. It is not an unfamiliar view. The domes have stood like that, shadowed, for the last fifty years. Those residences are Vega's constant reminder of all that was lost to him.

Until now.

Vega grins as he sails past the buildings. They won't be dark for much longer. Soon there will be females again.

Vega pulls his wings close and propels himself over the cliffs. He drifts across the abyss, savouring the feeling of freedom as he opens his wings to glide down into the indigo depths. A weight eases off

Vega's shoulders. This outcome has been a long time in the planning. It has taken a lot of preparation, not only the research into genetic enhancement but also the means to safely secure female dragon eggs.

A dangerous business. Dragon mothers do not normally give up their eggs willingly.

The thought snags again in Vega's mind and causes him to pause. Why did this Amberwing mother, this Ketu, so readily give up her eggs? The merpeople have been covertly scouring the mainland for the last two years, trying any means possible and without luck, to secure female eggs of any dragon breed.

Vega suddenly feels uneasy. He didn't question it before, but he wonders *how* the Amberwing heard of their need for eggs. Empress Naia's people are consummate professionals in the art of acquirement and smuggling—no rumour would have left their lips…

A strange scent catches in the back of Vega's gills and draws his attention away from thoughts of dragons. He glances upward. His senses, heightened in his natural form, search for the elusive smell again.

He finds it.

Blood.

Blood in the water.

Vega turns in a slow loop, long fins rippling back across his body as he searches for a direction. North, he decides. He straightens out and like a comet streaks back over the cliffs and towards the warmer waters closer to the mainland—closer to the merpeople's city of Amorpha.

Half a league from Ocerei, Vega finds Naunet. The merwoman, her fish-like tail now morphed back into place, is floundering. A deep cut mars her waist, the blood blossoming, cloud-like, in the water and tingeing it red. Her silver laser trident, a gift from the Hydraclaw's weapon laboratories, is held firm in her white-knuckled grip. A giant shark circles her, the blunt-nosed animal seeking an opening to strike.

Naunet, although injured, stares the creature down. Every line of her body is loose and ready. A capable warrior. She bares her teeth. Her fingers shift marginally, brushing the control button on the shaft of the trident. The tips of the weapon glow red, the laser energy within ignited and ready to fire. Naunet lunges forward. Three pinpoint blasts of light catch the shark on the side of its head. The animal slews sideways, charred skin scored parallel to its gills. Not yet defeated, it circles back.

But this time Vega is waiting.

At the sight of a massive Hydraclaw, the shark concedes defeat. No longer at the top of the food chain, it tips its powerful fins and propels off into the blue distance.

Naunet circles and catches sight of Vega. Her eyes widen, their green colour even more startling surrounded by the blueness of the ocean. 'King Vega?' she asks.

'Yes.'

Naunet crumples, all the strength she showed facing down the shark gone. 'They attacked without warning. My entourage is all but gone!'

Vega moves in closer to her. He morphs his left-hand fin into a long, whip-like strap and curls it reassuringly around her wrist. 'Calm yourself. Tell me what is happening?'

The merwoman points towards the surface where the sunlight colours the underside of the waves white. 'The acid-spitters. Amberwings. They claim the Accords between human and dragon were broken when eggs were stolen, and that we have sided with humans by trading those eggs!'

Vega hisses. 'But you said the eggs were donated.'

'They were, my Lord. The Amberwing's keeper gave them to us.' Naunet blinks. 'But now I fear treachery.'

Vega's mind whirls. Sundered Accords will mean a return to the old days—a time without law, when the different species of the world hunted each other to almost extinction. It is not an existence Vega wishes revived.

But he can't return the eggs to settle the Amberwing's ire either. Lorn's work will already be too far underway.

Naunet glances upward again. 'Please. My kin are being slaughtered up there. Will you aid me?'

The course of the future has been set. Picking a side is all that remains, and the Naia Clan has never failed him. Vega is not about to fail them.

'Lead the way,' he says.

***

The first sign of battle is the body of a dead Amberwing floating beneath the waves. It hangs suspended in the water. Its legs, not made for swimming, point uselessly to the sky and the wings curl upward, two drowned, golden scythes. Vega steers clear of the corpse, his eye trained on the waves that churn above him.

Vega shies to the left as a silver torpedo spearheads into the water. It is one of the merpeople's huge flying fish. A merman in humanoid form clings to its back, another laser trident held in his determined grip. He turns his fish expertly, a flash of glistening scales and opal fins, and then he is heading back, aiming for the sky.

Vega, with Naunet at his side, follows in the fish's slipstream. The water tastes dirtier as he gets closer to the surface—tastes of blood and acid. Bodies of merpeople and flying fish float on the surface, caressed by uncaring waves.

Vega breaches in a spray of foam and is momentarily blinded. The world is bright above the waves, a cacophony of blue sky, sunlight and red-tinged foam. He blinks, and his vision clears.

The battle is raging.

Five Amberwing dragons dominate the sky. Their great golden bodies are lined with teeth and claws, bodies that dip and dance out of the blue to rend at the remnants of Naunet's entourage. But the merpeople and their flying fish are not as delicate as they look. Lithe but quick, the remaining merpeople fight bravely. Their tridents are levelled. Red tracer lights burst from the tips of the weapons, pencils of death that speed between water and sky and collide with the armoured flesh of the sky dragons.

A scream. Vega turns. So does Naunet. The merman from before has been hit. As he tumbles from his fish, a huge, one-eyed female Amberwing dips to follow his fall. Naunet cries out, anguished, as the sky dragon catches him mid-air. One snap of her powerful jaws and he is consumed.

Vega's white-hot rage ignites. These dragons have no right! He opens his mouth and aims for the Amberwing. His breath may not be acid, but a Hydraclaw banshee scream is just as effective.

His blast of supersonic breath hits the Amberwing head on. The sky dragon's flight wobbles but her wing beats steady before she hits the water. Another dragon, slightly smaller than the first, is not so lucky. Closer to the waves, Vega's breath has unsettled her rhythm. Vega feels no small amount of satisfaction as the animal plunges into the water and struggles for a moment before her bulk drags her down.

The one-eyed Amberwing turns. Her black-opal eye swirls in anger, her teeth drip with acid venom. Vega's death hangs reflected in the set of her face.

'DESIST!' he screams over the tumult of waves, wind and battle cries. The Amberwing hesitates and Vega calls out again. 'Why do you attack?'

The sky dragon shrugs off a last laser bolt from one of the retreating merpeople. Her wings billow wide as she catches the wind to hover. 'Turn away, Hydraclaw,' she says. 'We claim rightful justice here. These merpeople are thieves. They have traded eggs stolen from us by humans.'

A wave tasting of acid slaps Vega in the side of the face. He shakes his head. 'Then your battle is with the humans,' says Vega. 'Not my merpeople.'

The Amberwing queen sneers, her lips rising to reveal her sharpened teeth. '*Your* merpeople? So am I conversing with King Vega then?'

'You are.'

The Amberwing huffs out an acid-laced breath, the scent of it stolen away on the salty breeze. 'Well, Last King of your Kind, hear me. The Accords are broken. The mainland has been taken, and the humans and their colluders are being dealt with. But as you are kin to my kind, I will grant you a concession. I bid you to go back to that watery grave you call a city, and we will allow you and your kind to linger there until you perish. I, Queen Ketu, claim the sky and all other lands.'

'Ketu?' whispers Naunet, floating by Vega's ear. 'My Lord, she is the queen who gave us the eggs!'

Vega frowns, his mind working to connect the pieces. 'Queen Ketu. You say eggs were stolen. Were they yours?'

The Amberwing's eye swirls, catching rainbows of fractured light in its depths. 'No,' she says, 'The eggs belonged to a sister. It is for her we seek retribution.'

It is Vega's turn to sneer, the sunlight glinting off his iridescent teeth. 'No,' he says. 'Retribution has nothing to do with it. You are seeking power.' The pieces of the puzzle fall into place. 'You engineered the breaking of the Accords, not the humans! But why?'

Ketu's nose wrinkles with disdain. 'Because a dragon's prerogative is to dominate the weak.'

'Ignorance is weakness,' replies Vega, 'and your actions define you as more ignorant than most!'

The sky dragon's jaw bunches in affront. Her wingbeats hasten and her eye swirls faster, a dark rainbow in her sunlight-coloured face. 'Your opinion is irrelevant, water worm. The truth is I have already won. The world is mine.'

'Today, perhaps. But tomorrow is uncertain. I deem your reign unacceptable. You will be challenged.'

'Not if you are dead, Vega,' roars Ketu. Viper-fast, her lower jaw drops and the acid sacs behind her tongue swell. She barks, sending a torrent of acid shooting past her lips.

Naunet screams as the fluid sheets across her. Vega turns away in time to save his eyes, but his neck takes the brunt of the hit. The length of it burns where his scales are scalded. Vega drops back beneath the waves. Around him, the last remaining flying fish with their riders school in close. Vega reaches out and curls his fin around Naunet. She is unconscious, her weapon fallen from lax fingers. He pulls her close then dives, speeding up to lead the others away from the Amberwings and their dreadful purpose.

***

Ocerei crests the horizon. The glittering domes are a welcome sight for Vega, whose wounds have sapped more energy than he wishes to admit. Naunet has still not moved. He pulls her closer to him.

Vega's mind races. Other than his people participating in the Accord War at the behest of the Empress Naia, Hydraclaws have never had much to do with the world topside. All their technology has been held close, too dangerous to be shared in the pre-industrial societies that dwell under the sun. But that may have to change. For a world where his daughters can grow in peace, Vega may need to join humanity in its fight against Ketu and her Amberwings.

The school of flying fish shoots forward, heading for the great entrance pool to the city. Vega, wearier than he has ever felt before, quickens his pace, eager to be home.

Lorn is waiting when they arrive. His cry of distress when he sees Naunet is all Vega needs to be convinced of his friend's love for her. Vega transforms back to his humanoid shape and lays the merwoman gently down on the floor. She still breathes but won't for long without help. He lets Lorn scoop her in his arms and carry her away in the direction of his lab.

Vega follows, but slowly.

It is warm and bright inside Lorn's lab. He has Naunet laid out on a table, the smell of antiseptics lingering in the air. Vega pauses by the merwoman's side. Her long tail fins are tattered, her arms and neck burnt raw with acid. Her face is still beautiful, but too pale. Lorn, standing opposite, looks just as colourless.

'Will she make it?' asks Vega.

Lorn shakes his head 'No. She's already gone.' His eyes paint a tragic portrait of loss—a portrait Vega is familiar with; one he saw many times in the mirror after his own wife was killed.

'I am sorry, old friend.'

'I never even told her how I felt about her.'

Vega recalls them together in the meeting room that morning, remembers the smile on Naunet's face. 'I don't think it matters, Lorn. I believe she knew.'

Lorn turns away from the table. He shrugs. 'I hope so.' Then, as if he no longer wishes to share his private pain, he changes the subject. 'There is something else I wish to show you.'

'What?'

'Come and see.'

Vega walks around the table, glad to be away from Naunet's still form. He follows Lorn to the long workbench where the eggs lie in an incubator. Except they are no longer eggs. Two tiny female dragons lie in the seaweed nest. Their small bodies are curled around on themselves as they sleep, tiny legs and fine, translucent butterfly wings twitching in their infant slumber. Their edges blur as they move, hinting at the morphing capabilities they will have upon maturation.

'They are blue,' says Vega, surprised.

'Yes.' A small sad smile touches the corner of Lorn's mouth. 'I claim artistic licence on that score.' He glances at Naunet then back at the hatchlings. 'They are the same colour as her hair.'

'Why not make them look like us?'

'Because they are not like us. They are hybrids and should have their own characteristics.'

'You are right.' An idea forms in Vega's mind. He tips his chin over to Naunet. 'Shall we name them for her? One Nau and the other Net?'

Lorn's face softens. 'I would like that.' His eyes flare bright as they fix on Vega. 'And I hope they grow to be like her, both decent and brave.'

Vega thinks on the uncertain times his daughters have been born into. 'They have no choice,' he whispers. 'They will need to be.'

SOULSLINGER:

DRAGON IN THE GUN

The saloon doors swing open with a creak. The noisome smells from inside the establishment roll with them—whisky, perspiration and tobacco. I wrinkle my nose. I hate this dusty, wild, sunburnt country. The Western Reach. I hate the dryness, the heat, and the bleached-white light. I especially hate the lack of civility. But I can't turn back. Not yet. My sister is missing, and I want answers.

My riding boots raise dust as I cross the worn timber threshold into the saloon proper. It's warmer inside the building, even though all the windows are thrown open. The bartender is busy polishing a glass. He stands behind the bar counter, a long, solid metal affair with copper pipes running vertically at equal spacings down the length. Every part of it gleams, well-polished. It looks out of place against the battered floor planks and the ramshackle walls. Condensation along the pipes reveals the bar to be refrigerated—a rarity this far past civilisation.

For an establishment that offers cold drinks, there is a distinct lack of patrons. Two men play poker by the far window. One bearded, one not. And a woman with a long black plait running down her back leans disinterestedly against the bar.

Nothing about the men warrants my further attention. Their worn boots and weathered skin suggest them to be prospectors or something of the like. But the woman is interesting. She is five parts human—Old World Native Indian descendant by the look of her—and one part, that being her right arm, artificial. The gears beneath the polished copper skin of her mechanical limb click each time she picks up her glass to drink. She almost looks like a man, in her plain shirt with rolled-up sleeves, vest, riding leathers and a black ten-gallon hat.

There is also a silver pistol holstered at her belt. But not just any pistol. I recognise the tech in the weapon. It's a sonic blaster; good for killing both sky dragons and rogue humans. It's one of my father's creations, King Vega of the Hydraclaw dragons. Our technologically advanced weaponry is second to none and used primarily to fight the sky dragons in their war against humanity.

And if the woman has a metal arm and a weapon like that, the Hydraclaws are not strangers to her. It's an interesting thought, and a possible opportunity if trouble presents.

I head for the bar. The bartender looks up at me. His eyes widen then slip away. I'm familiar with the reaction. Although I can morph away the details of my true dragon nature to seem human, my yellow eyes with their slitted pupils are a constant. But the man has no idea what I am, only that my eyes look predatory, so he moves to serve me.

'Wat canna getch ya?' he asks.

'Whisky with ice, and answers, if you've got them,' I reply.

The barman smiles, revealing broken, yellow teeth. 'The whisky's cheap. Answers—they'll cost ya.'

I pull a thick, gold coin out of my vest pocket. I place it on the bar.

The barman looks impressed. 'Good enough.' He tips the glass in his hand onto the counter, pulls a flexible metal hose up from beneath the bar, and from it lets three small spheres of ice clink into the glass. The frozen pieces fracture as a shot of warm whisky flows over them. The barman places the bottle back on the shelf. 'And now the answers?'

The two men playing cards stop to listen.

'I'm searching for a woman,' I say.

I hear a snigger. It's the poker player with the beard. 'Now a lass like yerself shoul' be looking for a man. I coul' help ya out. That there pretty blue hair of yers has righ' caught my fancy.'

I twist my head to look at the man. Turned so the barman cannot see me, I open my lips and smile, morphing my teeth into needle-sharp fangs. For extra effect, I fork my tongue and slither it out past them like a snake. 'Are you sure?'

Both men blanch and drop their cards. They rise to leave. Guns—normal human guns—hang holstered at their hips. My estimation of them changes; the men are gunslingers, not prospectors. I morph my teeth and tongue back into a less frightening aspect and wink at Beard Man as he passes me by.

The barman looks confused at the men's sudden departure. I pick up the glass and drink the whisky in one gulp, relishing the mix of alcohol burn and ice as it slides down my throat. I place the glass back down.

'So,' I say, tapping my fingernail on the gold coin. 'The woman. Blue hair like mine. Seen her?'

The barman picks up the glass. 'I seen 'er,' he says. 'Few weeks back. She came in 'ere lookin' for the Tinkerwitch.'

'Tinkerwitch?'

'Yeh. A crazy old bat that deals in alternative tech. Steam, wind power, that kinda stuff. Your woman said somethin' 'bout wantin' to buy some kinda dragon weapon off 'er.'

My sister was here trying to recruit gunslingers into soldier service—their skills being second to none as snipers to take down warring sky dragons. Why was she looking into weapons? 'Did you tell her where to find this Tinkerwitch?'

'Yeah. Up on Bloodstone Mesa, livin' up there in them cliffs.'

'Bloodstone Mesa?'

The barman points out the window to a distant, flat-topped mountain. It huddles squat against the stark horizon, its edges shifting and blurring in the heat haze rising off the prairie.

'Thank you.' I push the gold coin closer to him.

***

The sun has moved past high noon, but it's still hot outside. The main street is deserted, as if everyone is trying to avoid the heat. Even the buildings look wilted—such a different environment from my underwater home, the ocean city of Ocerei.

I head down the road that makes up the centre of town. Bloodstone Mesa broods in the distance, calling to me. I wonder if Net is still there, if she is alive. A part of me thinks that as her twin, I would somehow know if she were dead. Right now, I don't feel any different inside. I cling to the thought.

My horse, Mako, is corralled up at the blacksmith's. My preference would be not to take him to the mesa, but I have no choice. I can't risk flying these skies in dragon form and drawing unfriendly fire.

Mako nickers as I approach, ambles over to the fence and pushes his long, brown nose into my hand. He is after the carrots I ran out of a week ago.

'I have nothing,' I say. He huffs a hay-scented breath against my chest. 'Yes, I *will* have to do better next time.'

Mako is saddled and ready. One final check on the stirrup lengths, and I hoist myself up onto his back. I lean over and slap his neck. 'Let's go find Net,' I whisper.

But Mako rolls his eyes and sidles to the left.

Then a clicking noise starts up behind us.

I turn. It's the native woman from the saloon. She is leaning against the corner of the smithy, lightly tapping her mechanical fingers on the holster of her blaster. The brim of her hat conceals the woman's eyes. Her long plait hangs over the front of one shoulder. 'You look just like her,' she says.

I don't like the way she is caressing the gun. 'Like who?' I ask.

'The woman you were asking about back there—Net. That *is* who you are looking for?'

'You know her?'

'Yes. She enlisted me a few months back. We have been travelling together, headed for Amorpha. A city on the coast.'

Amorpha—City of the Merfolk ruled by Empress Naia. Allied with King Vega in the Sky Dragon War. Naia has the human garrison stationed there, concealed amongst the ruins on the foreshore cliffs. 'I am familiar with Amorpha. Do you know where my sister is?'

The woman pushes herself away from the wall. Her hand drops from her blaster. Her metal fingers stop clicking. She lifts her head. Her eyes, when they emerge, are black and diamond-hard; a hardness I have come to associate with the more-than-capable type of gunslingers. A no-nonsense fighter. Net made a good choice.

The woman tips her chin towards Bloodstone Mesa. 'The barman did not lie. Net left two weeks ago. She gave no details, only said I was to stay and await her return.'

'Why didn't you go looking for her?'

'I have,' replies the woman. 'She paid me a lot of gold to wait for her, but she is my friend, also. So I went. I did not find her. But there is something else out there you may have an interest in.'

An uneasy feeling crawls up my spine. 'You got a name?'

'Ojinjintka, but call me Ojin.'

I nod. 'I'm Nau. Saddle up. Show me what you found.'

***

The town lies far behind us, a tiny speck on the horizon. The yellow prairie circles us like rumpled corn silk. On our approach to the mesa's steep cliffs, Ojin slows her grey gelding to a trot. I follow her lead.

Up close, the precipices are a patchwork of red and yellow stone. The colours are a sharp contrast to the clear blueness of the sky overhead and the pale grass of the plain behind. A deep cleft, cleverly hidden behind a fold of stone, cuts back into the mesa. The fissure looks uninviting, strung through with loose boulders, rock spider webs and stunted bushes.

'We go through there?' I ask.

Ojin's lip curls, but there is no mirth in it. 'The spirits of the mesa will not hurt you. They are offended by what lies beyond,' she says. 'They will let us pass to right the wrong.'

I'm not sure I want to know what 'wrong' could be bad enough to offend spirits.

As we enter the cleft, Mako shies away from the close walls, snorting as his rump brushes the stone. The ravine widens slightly just past the opening. It rises a hundred metres on each side, the walls curving and bending back upon themselves to conceal the sky. Only a dim glow of sunlight filters down, touching briefly the higher portions of rock. But at least it is cooler in here. I loosen the top button of my shirt, grateful for the small reprieve.

Minutes pass along with endless stone and gloom. Echoes, awoken by the horses' hooves, bounce around us. I wonder if anyone else is listening to the sounds of our approach.

Ojin riding point, turns. 'Ready yourself,' she says.

The smell hits me even before we reach the exit. I gag, pressing my hand against my nose and mouth. We emerge from the ravine onto a small platform of rock that overlooks a bowl-shaped clearing. The area is carved from the heart of the mesa. Its walls are rugged and worn, dotted with clusters of elegant stone spires. The sky arcs innocently overhead.

But all beauty ends there.

The clearing—it's a boneyard.

A dragon boneyard.

I count at least thirty bodies in various states of decay, and countless other skeletons scattered about. All species lie tumbled together. Amberwing, Shattershrew, Glamourwing…

My palms break out in a sweat. My hands tremble. I search each body, forcing myself to note the grisly details. My gaze shifts past half-rotted hides—gold, silver and peacock green…

But no sapphire blue.

Net is not amongst the dead.

My heart's frantic tattoo slows. Ojin's face is grim, but she seems steeled to the tragedy below. Then I remember she has been here before.

'What is this place?' I ask. 'Who did this?'

'I do not know. I suspect the witch.'

Ojin's mention of the Tinkerwitch seems to flip a switch deep in the mesa. Heavy rumbling grinds out from the cliffs on the opposite side of the clearing, then a high-pitched wail shears the atmosphere.

The sound turns my blood to ice. Something shifts in my chest, a shift that leaves a sudden, hollow feeling, even as the noise fades. Silence follows.

Then, from high above the spires across the way, a large white cloud belches out of a hole in the cliffs.

Steam.

The Tinkerwitch.

'That did not happen last time I was here,' says Ojin.

I raise an eyebrow. 'Shall we go and see what it was?'

'Only the spirits could stop me.'

***

I wonder if Ojin is even capable of smiling. She is all business as she leads the horses back into the ravine and secures them there. Her blaster is in her mechanical hand when she returns.

'You any good with that thing?' I ask her as she stops to survey the clearing.

She holds the blaster up. Her eyes glitter like chipped coal. 'Let us hope you do not have to find out.'

A thin track weaves through the stone spires that encircle the clearing. I am thankful we can avoid walking amongst the dragon bodies. But even at a distance, the small details catch my attention—a silver Shattershrew lying on his side; the corkscrew-shaped skull distinctive and sharp-edged wings a mess of whitened bone and torn wing leather.

Another one, a smallish, mostly decayed Amberwing, lies with empty eye sockets and ivory teeth clenched—that one did not die easily. I swallow the bile that stings the back of my throat and refocus on the path.

One step. Two steps. The gravelly earth shifts beneath my boots. A hawk perched on the cliffs above us whistles out his keening call, and a lizard slithers back into its rocky abode. It is a wonder life exists in a place filled with such death.

Ojin stops. Her warm, human hand grasps my wrist. She presses a metal finger to her lips. I stop and listen.

The creak of unoiled wheels.

The snort of a horse.

I don't see them at first, but when I do, I recognise the gunslingers from the saloon. The two men are concealed by shadows as they lead a team of four horses from a cave mouth in the cliffs. Dragged by the animals is a long, flat cart on wheels. A large shape rests on the rolling platform—a dragon, nondescript and unmoving in the shadows. Then the men step into the sunlight.

Beard Man leads the horses, three bays and a black.

The cart clears the gloom—

And on it lies a sapphire-blue dragon, it's head half severed from its neck.

Net.

Dead.

A roar begs to leave my throat, but the sound is cut short. Ojin's swift hand clamps over my mouth. Her cold, metal fingers dig into my skin. I struggle against her. She's strong, but I am stronger. I refuse to be denied my rightful rage, so I loosen the hold on my human form. I begin to morph, letting my arms thicken and my teeth lengthen.

Then Ojin slaps me hard across the cheek. 'You can't help her,' she hisses, 'But we can avenge her if you keep your head!'

I stop, barely able to see her for the red haze that clouds my vision. How dare she strike me—how dare she ask me to stop? My sister has been murdered! My poor father will be devastated, and what of Net's eggs waiting for her back in Ocerei, the children who will never know their mother?

Ojin's eyes flare with a fire darker than their colour. Something in their depths resonates with me—Ojin understands my pain. She points at the men. 'A long time ago, white men like those slaughtered my family also. It is not right. You deserve your anger. You deserve revenge. But let us do it the right way.'

Through my grief, I recognise in Ojin a kindred spirit.

And realise why she never smiles.

I take a shuddering breath. My body is still fluid, fluxing—stuck halfway between human and dragon. My eyes lock onto Ojin's. She points at the corpses lying in the sunlight. 'Already so many dragons dead,' she says. 'This fight may be better fought in your two-legged form.'

She is right. My body settles, my human shape resolves itself. 'You know what I am?'

Ojin tips her chin towards the men now unceremoniously dumping Net's body alongside the others. 'I know what your sister was. I saw her change shape. I assume you are the same.'

'The same. Yes,' I whisper.

***

Ojin bids me to wait. I lean back on the lee side of one of the spires, hidden from view. I refuse to look at my sister's body, refuse to acknowledge her death. Instead I turn my gaze to the empty sky and try to focus.

We remain concealed until the men finish their grisly task. I peer around the rock spire as they lead the horses and cart back into the cave. I ease my blaster out of its holster. Ojin steps out from her hiding place.

We keep low as we sprint towards the cave, moving silently and clinging to the shadows. The entrance looms much larger than it looked from the distance. Tall and dark, it is more than wide enough for a dragon to be wheeled out on the cart. The stone threshold is well worn, marked heavily with wheel tracks.

An unfamiliar smell leaks out from the entrance. Scents belonging to damp places and also smoke, but not the good, clean scent of burning wood. A dirtier smell. I wrinkle my nose, take a breath and enter.

Inside the cave, the air is humid, so different from the dryness of the prairie. My eyes, designed for the dark depths of the ocean, make out the rough-hewn passage leading further into the cave. I nod to Ojin and she falls into step behind me.

The details of the path emerge with stone walls weeping moisture and a worn floor. At regular spacings, gas lamps, fixed to the walls, throw circles of yellow light. As we travel deeper, the sound of machinery at work grows louder. We turn a corner. The passage ahead is suddenly flooded with light.

An echoing voice screeches out commands. 'Get me more coal, you lazy braggarts!'

I ease back against the passage wall. Ojin's chest presses warm against my arm as she leans in to whisper. 'The main cavern must be ahead.'

I don't have time to answer. The sound of approaching footsteps grows louder. I push Ojin back against the wall and stand facing her. I shift my molecules, changing the colour of my skin to match that of the stone background. I hope whoever is coming won't notice my dark clothes against the rock.

Face to face with Ojin, I hold my breath. The gunslingers round the corner carrying a box with a shovel banging around inside of it, black and dirty looking. They pass by. Before I can stop her, Ojin steps around me, blaster in hand.

One man falls to the ground with a dent in his skull. The box and shovel fall with him. The other turns, hand on gun, but trips over his companion's legs. He lands hard, his eyes widening as he catches sight of Ojin.

She doesn't hesitate. A sonic blast ripples out silently from the muzzle of her blaster. The man arches and then slumps back—dead.

'It looks like you can use that blaster,' I say.

Ojin, for the first time, smiles.

And for some reason, I find it terrifying.

***

The Tinkerwitch's chamber is three dragons high and at least ten wide. A machine the size of a train car dominates the centre of the room. Without a skin, its mechanical innards are exposed to view, an intricate interplay of gold and silver cogs designed to spin a delicate, silver filigree box in the centre.

Different coloured pipes—gold, silver and copper—feed off a stationary plate at the base of the box, all heading in different directions. The silver ones reach up towards the ceiling, ending in a wide funnel that connects to the chimney outside. The gold all fix to a dragon-sized, metal cage with a glass globe fitted above it. Energy crackles in those pipes. The copper ones lead from the machine to a large, bowl-shaped metal bladder—a water bladder fixed above a forge.

Fire and water heated to boiling equals steam.

Steam power.

A fire rages in the furnace. Red light spills from it, illuminating the cave. The hiss of steam building in the silver pipes sounds like bees swarming. Ojin points towards the forge.

I missed her the first time. The Tinkerwitch. Small and wizened, she stands by the firebox at a control panel pulsing with yellow lights. Her dirty white hair hangs in dreadlocks so long they brush the floor—a floor painted filthy with coal dust. Coal. So that is the source of the unclean smoke smell.

The witch taps at a gauge. 'Not hot enough, not hot enough,' she mumbles to herself.

I unholster my blaster and step into the cavern. My grip is steady on the weapon my father built for me. I call out. 'Step away from the machine.'

The Tinkerwitch doesn't turn, but she starts to laugh—a cold, cruel cackle that sets my teeth on edge. 'Welcome, welcome,' she says, the rhythm of her voice fast-paced and breathy. 'Of course I knew you were coming. The boys said they saw you at the saloon. Saw the way you changed your shape.' Then she turns. Her eyes, glowing red, fix on mine. 'You are like *her*, aren't you? The blue one? Yes, of course you are. You have the same colouring in your hair as she did. She was special, that one. That's why, when I heard you were coming, I moved her up the harvest list. Couldn't risk losing her.'

Horror coils through my belly. I recall the teeth I flashed at the gunslingers in the saloon. I revealed myself to them, my true nature, and in that moment condemned my sister to an early death.

Ojin steps up beside me. Her mechanical arm and blaster both glint wickedly in the firelight as she lines the Tinkerwitch up in her sights. 'What are you doing here, Witch?'

The Tinkerwitch seems unperturbed. She picks up a shovel and scoops another pile of coal into her forge. The fire flares. 'I am a weapons designer,' she says, putting the shovel back down.

'What have dragons got to do with that?' I ask.

The Tinkerwitch smiles, her teeth black stubs in her mouth. 'I am so glad you asked.' She abruptly stabs at a yellow-lit control button. There is a rumble, a creak of chains and sudden *whoosh* of air.

A cage falls from the ceiling, trapping us.

***

The Tinkerwitch stands several feet away, examining us. I snarl at her, not caring that my face is shifting, and that my claws are lengthening.

'Good. Excellent,' says the witch. 'I'll want you in your dragon form to harvest you in any case, so may as well change now.'

Unwilling to accommodate her need, I stop. My shape settles halfway between human and dragon—human except for long teeth and claws retained. But I'm still reluctant to concede defeat. I cannot use my dragon breath while in my current form, but I have my blaster. I raise it to the cage bars, my finger on the trigger.

'Energy-based weapons like those won't work in there,' says the witch. 'The cage is fortified against them.' She points up.

I follow the line of her finger and see more articulated copper pipes running from the main machine and connected to the roof of the cage. I frown and lower the gun. 'What exactly do you intend to harvest from me?'

The Tinkerwitch smiles again. She turns to look lovingly at her steam-driven contraption. 'With my Soul Harvester, I'll take your soul.'

'My soul?' I ask.

'Dragon souls are the best source of raw energy in the universe. Highly sought after as powering mechanisms for new weapons.'

New weapons? My mind spins. King Vega provides the only source of advanced munitions on the planet. 'My father would never condone the use of dragon souls! He will not buy them from you. We want to win the Sky Dragon War, but not like that!'

'Your father?' replies the witch. 'Oh, you mean King Vega?' She laughs, a wet cackle that rattles out of her throat. 'He means nothing to me. Stupid dragon. You really have no concept as to how small your existence is, do you?' She turns away as if disgusted. 'Your sister was just as ignorant and arrogant as you.' She sniffs. 'Your world—Eridan— is only important because dragons exist here, and only here. Nowhere else in the universe.' She shakes her head. 'There is so much more going on, up there in space, than you could ever comprehend.'

Ojin leans against the cage bars. Her blaster hangs loosely from her mechanical hand. With a minute tip of her chin, she gestures to it; her eye flicks towards the old woman.

She wants me to bait the Tinkerwitch into stepping closer.

I can do that.

'Then tell me,' I say. 'Educate this "stupid" dragon.'

The Tinkerwitch's mouth screws up into a knot. 'There is another war raging in the darkness above this planet,' she says. 'A war for power. Aliens all fighting to claim your world. Some of them wish to save dragonkind, but my people—the Tinkervaatch— we wish to harvest you into weapons and use you to dominate the universe.'

Ice crawls down my spine. A poor end for dragonkind. 'And how do you intend to succeed?' I turn my nose up at her. 'I see nothing extraordinary when I look at you.'

The insult is enough to prick her vanity. She wants me to know how clever she is. The Tinkerwitch rolls her neck, and I hear it crack. Then she reaches into her filthy jerkin and pulls out a gleaming, golden pistol. A clear canister is fitted where the bullet cylinder should be.

In the canister swirls a clear blue spark of light.

I don't need her to tell me what it is.

I would recognise my sister anywhere, in any form.

And that is her soul in the gun.

'Taming dragons is no great feat,' snarls the Tinkerwitch. 'I just put one in the Extractor.' The witch points the gun to the cage on her machine. 'I separate the soul with steam molecules and collect it up there.' She points to the glass globe above the cage, then swings the gun to point at the forge. 'Then I melt that soul into the gold that becomes the weapon. Any weapon you like. And there is no need for bullets. The dragon's spirit energy not only increases the power of the weapon ten thousand-fold, but as ammunition, it is infinite. It returns to the gun. Reusable energy.' The witch smiles as if proud of herself. 'I can blast a starship out of space, even with a small shooter like this.' The witch steps forward and leans in, her face pressed close to the cage bars, 'And you, my dear, are going to join your sister. I've always wanted a matched pair of pistols.'

The stock of Ojin's blaster falls with a sharp crack on the Tinkerwitch's temple. The old woman sways, looking confused as she touches the blue-green blood trickling down her cheek. Then Ojin reaches through the bars and locks her metal hand around the Tinkerwitch's throat.

The alien woman doesn't die without a fight. Her iron-hard fingernails scrape down Ojin's mechanical arm, sending sparks to the ground. She kicks and twists with surprising strength. Ojin clenches harder.

The mechanisms in her arm click louder, increasing in tempo—

Then the Tinkerwitch falls still. Her fingers slip away from Ojin's arm, her eyes stop moving, and her mouth falls lax.

Ojin drops the limp corpse to the ground. It falls like a bundle of sticks. She takes a breath and wipes her metal fingers clean down the front of her shirt. 'The spirits will deal with her now,' she says.

***

It takes a while, but the coal-fed flames in the forge burn down. Without fire to fuel the steam, the witch's Soul Harvester stops running. Without power, the door to our cage springs open.

I step out. The cavern is gloomier without the brightness from the furnace, but wall lamps, like those in the passage, provide just enough illumination.

Ojin slides past the silent Harvester, looking to explore another corridor that leads deeper into the cavern system. I remain, considering the gleaming metal machine that killed my sister. The Soul Harvester. Every part of me wants to tear the metal monster apart, piece by piece, to avenge my sister.

But where to start?

The Tinkerwitch's gun. It lies half hidden beneath the fall of her dirty skirts. I kick the filthy fabric away, revealing the weapon. Its golden casing glows in the uncertain light, the spark in the pistol's clear barrel flickers. I reach down and pick it up. But as soon as I touch it, the metal in the gun whispers to me.

'Nau?'

My sister's voice.

'Net?'

The spark dances urgently in the canister. Nau's touch on my mind grows stronger. *'Yes, sister.'*

My heart leaps. 'But how?'

'I am not dead. I have been changed.'

Tears sting my eyes. I choke back a sob and cradle the golden gun to my chest. 'I'm sorry I failed you.'

'You did not fail me, sister. I made my own mistakes.'

'What mistakes?'

Net pauses. *'I came here alone, and alone is never the answer.'*

I process that thought. 'What do we do?'

'A war is being waged for our souls, Nau. Amongst the stars above us. We need to go there, find our allies and fight for all dragons.'

'But father needs us.'

'Father has others to help him. Dragonkind on the other hand—'

'What difference will we make?'

'We can join the battle. We find those who fight for us and help them win.'

'How?'

'The Tinkerwitch's vessel lies hidden in these caverns. We take the other dragon guns and her ship to the stars.'

'You want to take on beings from other planets!'

'Yes. Get me close enough, and I can destroy them all if you have the courage to wield me.'

My sister has always been the stronger twin. Determined, bold and indomitable. And she has always been right. I'll not turn away from her now.

As my resolve strengthens, she speaks again. *'I claim you, Nau, and I name you anew. No longer* Hydraclaw, *you are now* Soulslinger. *I am your weapon and you are my body. Now aim me, fire me and I will show you what we can achieve together!'*

I do as my sister asks. I lift and aim. I press my finger to her trigger.

It clicks.

A blast of blue, dragon-shaped energy erupts from her barrel. I stumble backwards with the force of it. The smell of heat-stressed air circles me as Net burgeons forward and encompasses the Soul Harvester. I see a flash of teeth and the line of a butterfly-shaped wing in the brilliance of her soul's light.

The metal pipes of the Harvester begin to glow red. They hold their shape for an instant then melt, falling in great, gleaming drops to the floor. My sister's ghostly laughter echoes around me as she moves on to the forge. Then the Tinkerwitch. Net swoops on her corpse. Soon nothing remains but a smear of greasy ash on the scorched stone.

And all the while, I stand unharmed.

***

Net returns, with an air of self-satisfaction, to her canister just as Ojin steps clear of the far passage. With a wide-eyed stare, the Indian woman looks at the ruined machine. 'What did you do?' she asks.

'It wasn't me. My sister. She lives on in the gun.'

Ojin's eyebrows rise. 'Still alive? And you fired her? We could have just dismantled the machine.'

'My sister had every right to destroy it.'

'I am pleased she is still with us.' Ojin's lip quirks up then she pulls another golden pistol from behind her back. 'There is a whole armoury back there. Your father may find them useful in helping to end his war.'

'My father is a moral dragon. He would never touch those guns. But I will take them.'

Ojin's brow furrows. 'Where?'

'My sister wishes to join the war the Tinkerwitch spoke of.' I point up, indicating the sky, hidden past the cave's ceiling. 'I am going with her.' I shrug. 'If you were interested in a change of occupation, you could come with us.'

'And become a Soulslinger?'

A shiver runs up my spine at Ojin's use of the word. 'What do you know of Soulslingers?'

Ojin's face turns apologetic. She looks at the pistol in her hand. 'I am sorry, Nau. When I touched it…the dragon within spoke. She claimed me, said I am her *Soulslinger*. I…I pledged myself to her.' Ojin's gaze fixes back to mine. 'By the spirits, Nau, this one is so full of anger. She is—was—an Amberwing. Her own kind betrayed her. They stole her children then gave her to the Tinkerwitch. She has suffered such loss. She is a mirror to my own spirit.'

I consider the gun in Ojin's hand—a gun so like Net. In its chamber floats a golden spark, the colour of an Amberwing's hide. My sister's voice whispers in my mind. *'There is no changing it. Ojin belongs with us now.'*

And again my sister is right. I tip my chin up. 'Being a Soulslinger will suit you well, I think.'

Ojin smiles, and it is every bit as terrifying as before. She cradles her new gun in both hands. 'We will fight alongside you.' Her smile changes into a full grin. 'To whatever end.'

I nod, both relieved and glad for her choice. 'And does the dragon in your gun have a name?' I ask.

Ojin looks down at the weapon. She traces a gentle finger across its glimmering lines. 'She calls herself Rahu.'

CHRONOHIDE: TOMB OF THE SAURIAN KING

There is something cold about this empty, ruined hall. Something about how the crumbling, salt-laced, stone walls open up to the watercolour sky and the way the waves sound as they crash against the cliffs outside. Amorpha. City of the Merfolk. Home to the Naia Clan. This is no place for a desert dweller like myself. But here I am. Waiting. I tap my fingernails on the stock of the gun holstered at my hip. A nervous habit. The soul of the dragon in the weapon's chamber, Argo, whispers to me. '*Steady, Jack. You can do this.*'

A gust of wind blows past me, carrying with it the iodine smell of seaweed. I glance up. Empress Naia enters from a side doorway, flanked by a white-haired human woman armed with a laser trident. I catch a brief glance of the view beyond the door—a framed view of the derelict stone city clutching at the cliffs. It looks deserted, but I know better. Those ruins house refugees displaced by the decades-long war against the sky dragons, and the human garrison that defends them.

The empress's silver hair ripples like a wave down her back. As it moves, the colour shifts, cycling through pale hues, metallic, like the inside of an abalone shell. Scales cover her skin from ankle to neck, shining like newly polished silver. But her beauty fades there.

The empress is ancient. Her cheeks are weathered dark by her years in the sun and by the tide. She walks upright but slowly, supported by a white whalebone cane. I don't fail to see the tremble in the human legs she has assumed for our meeting, the human legs that will have carried her from the rocky shoreline to this throne room.

Her guard takes up residence at the side of the throne. The empress does not rush as she settles herself upon it. The polished black granite seat, inlaid with swirling, wave-like lines of beaten gold, dwarfs her slim form. She leans her cane against her left leg then looks up at me.

Her pale, sea-green eyes are as sharp as knives. Full of wisdom, they bore into my soul, like a Shattershrew dragon bores through stone. When she speaks, her voice resonates with power. 'I detest being on land, so this better be good. Why are you here, Human?'

A tough audience. I swallow. I take off my hat and lift my chin. 'Empress Naia. I'm Jack Johns. I'm here with greetings from the Hydraclaw Dragon princesses, Nau and Net.'

The empress's chin jerks up sharply. Her eyes thin to daggers. 'The princesses? You lie. They are dead.'

I look down at my hat. I run the brim of it through my fingers. I remember Nau's hand on my shoulder as she said, *'Naia is as stubborn as old boots. It will not be easy to convince her, Jack. But you have to. For the sake of us all...'*

I look back up. 'No, ma'am. Not dead.' I reach into my pocket and pull out the lock of Nau's hair she gave me as proof of life. The blue colouring of it is unique. Unmistakable. I hold it up. The empress's eyes widen, and then thin again. I continue. 'Nau and Net have spent the last five years fighting an enemy far greater than anything you could imagine.'

'You speak of the sky dragons?' scoffs Naia. 'No. If the princesses live, then it is obvious they have abandoned us to our war. They are traitors.'

'No,' I say. 'They remain ever loyal to Eridan. I'm talking about a different enemy, one a great deal more dangerous than the dragons—this is about the Tinkervaatch.'

Naia's brow furrows. 'Tinkervaatch?'

I point up to the sky. The empress's eyes remain fixed on me. 'Aliens, ma'am. From space. They're coming. We have intel. They're looking for the ancient dragon you have buried under your city.'

Naia's good at concealing her thoughts, but not quite good enough. I don't miss the small rise of her eyebrow, the clench of her fists. But she's not giving up any secrets. 'Who are you?' she hisses.

I frown. 'I am Captain of Princess Nau's second regiment. She sent me to tell you that we are on the verge of victory. We have the Tinkervaatch on the run. But they have discovered the legend of the Chronohide dragon. They want him—want him to take them back in time and avoid their defeat.'

Naia's lip curls up in disdain. The whitened points of her teeth press against the redness of her lips. The teeth of a Siren. 'The Chronohide is a myth. There is no such thing as a fire-breathing, time bending dragon. And there is certainly no tomb beneath my city.'

I get why she has to protect the secret. But I'm not a man to beg. My temper prickles. 'Look ma'am. I'm no good with pretty words. So I'll lay it straight. I'm telling you the truth. If you listen to me, we can save the world. If you don't—well, I'm gonna head home, get a bottle of strong whisky and a good seat to watch it all burn down. What's it gonna be?'

The empress looks offended. But then her fists slowly unclench, and her sneer turns into a genuine smile. 'Only Nau would know me well enough to send someone like you.' She arches her eyebrow. 'I have never been one to be bought with pretty words.' She turns to the female guard. 'Adeen, I will speak with him further in private. Please take him to my chambers.' She glances at me then back at the woman, 'And bring us the best bottle of whisky you can find.'

***

Empress Naia's chambers are lower down the cliffs, in a more intact part of the ruins. The room is small but well appointed, with a window that opens to the sea. In the distance, a string of emerald islands cling to the horizon. The chamber also boasts a domed ceiling painted with an underwater ocean scene. I marvel at the minute detail on the dolphins that cavort alongside long-fingered corals and the more sombre presence of gilt-toothed sharks.

Two heavy chairs, upholstered in teal and green, huddle around a small, dark timber table sitting atop a thick sheepskin rug. The butter-coloured floor covering is the only warmth in the room, all other decorative hues taken from an ocean-inspired palette. Two glasses and a crystal carafe filled with amber liquid wait on the table. The whisky.

'Please, sit down.' Naia's cane clicks on the floor as she enters the room. 'You have come a long way, no doubt.'

I nod and take the seat opposite the window. Naia places her cane against the other seat and leans over to uncork the whisky. She pours it neat into the glasses, takes one and hands the other to me. She sighs heavily as she sinks into her own chair, the whisky then downed in a single gulp.

I can't say the old lady doesn't impress me.

'My kind are long-lived,' says the empress. 'And when you get to be as old as me,'—she lifts her glass to look at it—'you really appreciate the small things in life. A fine whisky is one of those things.'

'I can't fault that thinking.' I lift my own glass and down my drink just as easily. I place the fine glass, finer than anything I have ever held before, back on the table. Its crystal edge catches the sunlight streaming in through the window and fractures it.

'Ma'am,' I say. 'I'd love to sit here and finish this bottle with you, and I'm real sorry to be pushy. But the aliens aren't waiting. What can you tell me about the Chronohide?'

Naia considers her glass for a moment longer. She looks up. 'I will help you because the Hydraclaw princesses are like daughters to me, and I am grateful for the news of them.' She shakes her head as if to clear old memories. Her voice grows stronger. 'I know a little of the Chronohide. He is a merfolk legend. Supposedly the first of all dragons and the only one of his kind, a fire-breathing Saurian King. But he is cursed—an immortal in that he can be tied by death but never contained by it. He can also bend time, travel back and forth across a period of the most recent five hundred years.'

'The Tinkervaatch prisoner we interrogated confirmed that,' I say. 'Is there anything else they wouldn't know?'

The empress's mouth twists into a shrewd smile. She leans forward conspiratorially. 'They wouldn't know that my great grandfather was the one to entomb him somewhere along this coast.' She pauses a moment, her eyes glittering. 'The location of the tomb was hidden from all, including my father—the Emperor—and myself.' She lifts a long, crabbed finger and points to a series of misshapen scales just above her left breast, 'But I was given the key to find it.'

'So…you have a map?'

'No. I didn't say a *map*. I said I had the *key*.'

***

The warped scales on the empress's chest are a brand placed there when she was a child. As I kneel by her side looking at them, the thought of it makes me sick. I branded plenty of Western Reach cattle back in the days before Princess Nau gave me a dragon-soul gun and made me a Soulslinger. I will never forget the stink of burning flesh, the screaming holler of the animal. What kind of sick bastard does that to their own kin?

Argo's touch is soft against my mind. '*Humans. Merfolk. Tinkervaatch…you are all the same, my friend, all barbarians in some way.*'

He isn't wrong.

The empress must also sense my discontent. She leans back from me and tilts her head. 'The brand is a mark of royalty, Jack, given to all heirs to preserve the key and ensure the Chronohide is never released. I assure you, the pain of it was brief, and the purpose vital.'

'Doesn't mean I have to like it,' I say. I put my hands on my knees and push myself upright. I point to the disfigured scales on her skin. 'And I know you said it was a key, but I'll be damned if those five marks along the top don't look like the islands outside your window.'

The empress's head snaps around to take in the view. 'Hah!' she says. 'You are right. I have never considered that before.' She peers down at the mark again. 'What of this final mark, the one shaped like the petals of a flower?'

I lean in to look again. Deciphering the island reference was easy. Five islands on the horizon outside her very window, five marks. But the other one, I can't imagine what it could be.

'It's the shape of a Shattershrew's tail,' says Argo. *'I had a tail like that—all earth dragons have tails like that! Perfect for carving through stone!'*

His excitement infects my mind. Adrenaline races through my blood, my heart begins to skip. For a moment I am lost in Argo's memories of his old life, the life he had before the Tinkervaatch harvested his soul and imprisoned him within the gun. Argo begins to shudder in his holster.

Naia notices it also. 'Why is your gun vibrating in your pocket like that?'

'It's a holster ma'am, not a pocket. And the gun is my dragon, Argo. He is telepathic. He's telling me the mark resembles a Shattershrew's tail—earth dragons—maybe they have something to do with the solution?'

'Wait. Your gun is a dragon?'

'Yes. A Shattershrew. His soul lives in my gun.'

The empress turns pale. 'A dragon's soul is in that gun?'

I frown. 'He's the reason I'm here, the reason we have to stop the Tinkervaatch. They did this to him and to many other dragons also.' I hesitate a moment then decide to tell her the truth. 'The Hydraclaw princess Net, Nau's sister, is tied the same way to such a gun. And that's what those bastard aliens want to do to all dragons. Kill their bodies and enslave their souls. That's why we need to find the Chronohide. We need to find a way to secure him to his death forever, before they can find and awaken him.'

Empress Naia looks as white as a sheet. 'Net? Princess Net's soul is in a gun?'

'Yes, ma'am. I'm sorry to say she is.'

A single tear crawls out past her pale lashes. She quickly wipes it away and nods—a nod that marks a resolution. 'For Net then,' she says. She lifts a finger to point at the last mark on her chest. 'And your dragon is right. I should have seen it before. The mark of a Shattershrew, along with the island reference. I think I know where to find the Chronohide's tomb.'

***

The small beach at the base of the cliffs is a wild, rugged place. My boots crack barnacles and slip on the black rocks that line the sand at the water's edge. Fierce waves batter the cliffs ahead, shattering against the stone and flinging foam into the wind. I wipe the sea spray from my face, not for the first time, and curse. But the empress is smiling. She seems in her element.

A desolate bluff, its edges worn to honeycomb, fences off the far end of the beach. This seems to be the empress's destination. She hastens as we approach it, finally stopping when we reach its crumbling foot.

Naia stares up at the far heights of the weathered cliff. Her hair and cheeks are crusted with droplets of shimmering water. This close to the ocean, her years fall away and she seems timeless. 'Look,' she says.

In the distance, the five islands are now aligned. From this angle, they form the rough outline of a Shattershrew dragon sleeping. 'And here.' Naia points to a vertical section of rock close to the waterline. As the waves recede on their outward path, a weathered carving is revealed, scored deep in the stone.

A flower-like design.

A Shattershrew's tail.

'This mark has been here for as long as I can remember,' says the empress.

I scratch at my day old beard. 'You think it marks the entrance to the tomb?'

'Could the answer be so obvious?'

In my experience, nothing is ever as easy as that. The oncoming waves rush around my boots as I approach the carving. I lean in to look closer. Small crabs and barnacles cling to the recesses of the mark, blurring the already worn edges. I trace the lines and crevices of the surrounding rock, but it's solid. I straighten, frustrated. 'There's no entrance here,' I call back to Naia.

Argo sounds amused as he whispers into my mind. *'The answer is there in front of you, Jack.'*

'If you know something, feel free to share it, Cowboy,' I reply in mind-speak.

My gun shifts in its holster—Argo's way of pointing. *'That mark decrees that only a Shattershrew can open the way. Unholster me, Jack. I'll clear the path for you.'*

A slow grin creases my lips. *'You are one clever bastard, Argo.'*

'I am a wise bastard,' he replies with a warm chuckle.

I pull the gun free. Argo's silver soul dances, a bright spark, in the clear canister built in where the bullet cylinder should be.

'What are you doing?' asks Naia, her gaze fixed on the gun.

'My dragon. He knows the way,' I reply. 'You might want to step back a little.'

But the empress is stubborn. She stands her ground. 'Suit yourself,' I say with a smile and pull the trigger.

Argo burgeons forth from the gun in a blast of silver light. His form shifts, coalescing to resemble the shape he was when living. His long, corkscrew-shaped head forms first, then the outline of a sharp-edged wing built for digging, the striking flower-shaped tail.

My dragon hits the stone with a sonic boom. The power of his soul, amplified by his connection to the gun, disintegrates the cliff face. Shards of rock shower down like rain, catching and cutting at my skin. The empress huddles over her cane, letting her back take the brunt of the debris. Then silence.

My ears are ringing. The air smells of molten stone and charred seaweed. But when I open my eyes, my heart leaps, forgetting all else. A round, smooth-walled passage has been cleared.

Argo has opened the way.

The Chronohide awaits.

***

Naia's staff is even more useful than I first realised. The whalebone glows in the dark, lighting our way as we enter the tomb. The sound of the waves crashing grows distant, muffled as we are swallowed by the dense rock. Everything smells of salt and ash.

Ancient pictographs line the walls of the passage. I survey them as I pass, the carvings depicting strange creatures made of light, men that walk on four legs, and merfolk riding whales like horses.

The Shattershrew depictions are easy to recognise. They're drawn in rows, all bowing to a dragon-shaped monster made of flame. The artist used fluid lines to suggest the shape of the creature, the contour of teeth and a broad wingspan, rather than an actual form. It's as though the illustrator was hesitant to define a true shape, as if by doing so, it would somehow become real. I shudder. Perhaps the artist knew something I don't.

The passage is not long. It angles sharply in towards the mainland for several metres, ending at a large, rusted iron door. Two unlit torches in sconces flank the closed entrance.

Naia raises her staff to look at the door. Markings are etched in the iron. 'This is ancient Amorphian,' she says. Then she leans in closer and begins to translate, 'Beware. Beyond, the future ends. Cursed is that which is bound here by salt and stone and cloth.

The Trinity of Creation to quell, Raw Life to raise The Fallen.'

'Sounds promising,' I say.

'Sounds like we should be turning back,' replies Naia, her face grim.

The iron door swings open on creaking hinges. The darkness beyond is heavy and thick, impenetrable even by the light of Naia's staff. She glances up, forlorn, at the torches next to the door. 'Having one of those alight would be useful about now.'

'I'm on it, ma'am.' I take one down and reach into my pocket for my flint. A spray of sparks and the end ignites. The acrid stench of sulphur and lime rises with the smoke.

The warm firelight precedes us as we enter the chamber. Naia's shuffling steps sound muffled against the stone floor. Her cane clicks as she leans on it. Her breathing is heavier also. The walk to the bluff has wearied her.

'There are more torches on the wall over there.' She points to her right.

I walk over and touch the burning brand to the closest one. It's as if I have flipped a switch. With the first, the rest of the torches follow, flaring into light and flooding the room with golden brilliance. My eye runs across the scene, an immense room dotted with smooth granite pillars and a ceiling hidden in darkness. The floor is littered with dragon bones, and the raised dais in the centre holds a giant corpse encased in salt-encrusted bandages.

An ancient mummy.

The Chronohide dragon.

'Dear Goddess of the Sea,' whispers Naia. She looks shocked as she takes in the lines of the mountainous beast. 'He is larger than any dragon I have ever seen.'

I point to the scattered bones around the room. The distinctive corkscrew-shaped skulls are obvious in the light. 'And it looks like the Shattershrew dragons were his followers,' I say. Argo touches my mind; he is curious but doesn't speak.

A ripple of unease shivers across the empress's shoulders. 'Let us be done here swiftly,' she says. 'This place is evil. I wish to be away.'

I'm not about to argue with her. A bad aura certainly clings to this place. I clip the torch I'm carrying into an empty wall sconce and head to the dais.

The details of the Chronohide are concealed behind its dusty wrappings, but even so, the points of wicked spikes are clear, pressing through the cloth next to the outline of a huge eye socket. The stone platform itself is simple. No carvings, just three small bowls polished into the surface at the edge. Dark brown sediment stains the bottom of each. I touch one, tentatively. The residue flakes and sticks to my fingers.

I turn to Naia. 'What did it say on the door outside? Something about a Trinity?'

'The Trinity of Creation to quell, it said, and Raw Life to raise The Fallen.'

I show her my fingers. 'I think there's blood in these three bowls.'

Naia frowns. 'It would make sense,' she says. 'Blood is of creation and there are three main species on our world—human, dragon and merfolk.' Naia turns her gaze back to the Chronohide's corpse. 'Perhaps that is the secret to his binding. A stone tomb, salted wrappings and the blood of the three.'

'How do we make sure the bind is permanent?'

Naia shrugs, but Argo answers. '*I think I can do it,*' he says. '*Enhanced by the gun, I should be powerful enough to incinerate his bones.*'

I glance down at Argo. His soul hangs motionless in his canister. Is it apprehension I sense coming from him? I glance around at the Shattershrew bones that line the walls. 'And if you are not?'

'*Then I will die trying.*'

'*Are you sure you want to do that?*'

'*Those dragons by the walls were not his followers; they were his slaves. They sacrificed themselves to bind him. Let me try and do this, Jack. For them.*'

'What are you thinking?' asks Naia, pressing up closer to me.

'Argo. He thinks he can destroy the bones.'

Naia's brow furrows. 'A drain like that on his power might kill him. I don't like it.'

'Neither do I. But it's his choice—unless you have a better idea.'

The empress steps back. She raises her chin. 'Your dragon is brave. Let him try.'

I pull Argo from his holster. His gold casing gleams in the firelight. His soul-spark is trembling in the canister. '*Ready?*' I ask.

'*Ready, Jack,*' he says.

Argo's soul lights the cavern like a small sun, blinding, as he exits the barrel to encompass the mummified dragon.

But as he touches the corpse, something turns awry. Instead of smelling bandages burning, I hear Argo scream. His ghostly wail shears through me like ice. My knees buckle and I hit the floor, blinded by his agony shared. Naia grips my arm, but her words are muffled. I wrench my eyes open against the pain. The room is dimmer than before.

Argo is battling for his life. His essence swirls around the Chronohide's skull, growing ever smaller as it seems to be absorbed through the wrappings and into the bone. Suddenly the eye socket glows a wicked green behind the cloth.

Then the Chronohide's corpse shifts.

The mighty skull rises from the dais. Spikes press against and tear through the coverings that hold his body together. The bindings collapse away to reveal a dragon half-built—bone stitched together with sinew and newly formed muscle. Patches of skin grow across his shoulders as Argo's spirit diminishes further.

'I'm sorry, Jack...'

'No!' I cry out as my dragon's life force flickers out.

Naia's nails dig into me like claws. Her voice grows clearer. 'On your feet!' she screams, dragging me up. The Chronohide, now with a fully formed head, roars a primal scream of rage. His head collides with the ceiling of the cavern as his wings tear away the last of his wrappings. Several columns tremble and crumble in their wake.

Together, we sprint back through the tunnel and onto the beach. The salt air hits me like a slap to the face as we exit. I stumble in the surf, but Naia hauls me upright again. She's stronger than she looks.

In moments, we are clear of the bluff and the surf. My gun is still in my hand, but the metal is now dull grey. Grief for Argo's loss punches me like a fist to the gut. 'What happened?' I sob.

Naia grits her teeth. 'We were stupid! That's what happened,' she snarls. 'We fed Argo's soul to that monster's bones—raw life to raise The Fallen. The Chronohide has used him to reclaim awareness!'

Another mighty roar causes me to look back. The Chronohide has crawled free of his tomb. He stands atop the bluff. His wings are held aloft, their edges alight with flames. His blood-red scales catch the last rays of the dying day and drip scarlet glints onto the cliffs below. His mouth opens, and a moment later a torrent of flame and black smoke bellows into the sky.

Then his eyes turn upon us, wicked green. In them I witness his elation.

I try to turn away, try to keep running, but it's no use. The Chronohide is already gathering strands of existence. The air bends around me, and Naia sobs. She too senses what is coming.

Then around us the world shifts.

Clouds skid rapidly across the sky in smears of colour. The sun rises and falls and rises again. I watch the sea recede and the cliffs rebuild stone long worn away. I see a blood-soaked beach littered with the bodies of sky dragons and merfolk. They fade to be replaced with a swarm of Shattershrew dragons branded and bound by chains. Then they too disappear.

The regrettable history of our world, Eridan, replayed.

Naia drags me around and pulls me back into a run. The movement is full of strength, her reflexes growing ever more certain. She is changing also. The years are falling away from her face; her hair is changing from abalone silver to emerald green.

Time.

Time is being bent backwards.

I crumble to the ground. Naia shouts again, but there's nothing she can do. She is long-lived. She exists in this older time—young but alive.

I do not.

I squeeze her hand, but my grip is weak.

My atoms are fraying apart.

'Don't you dare give up!' she yells. 'Get up!'

Renewed youth and strength have made her beautiful. What a last sight for a dying man to see. 'It's not over,' I whisper. 'The Tinkervaatch will come—you need to destroy the Chronohide.'

The light catches the tears on Naia's cheeks, turning them to diamonds. 'I won't let them win, Jack,' she whispers. 'I'll save the future and see you again.'

My atoms are all undone. My body starts to break apart—feet and legs disintegrating to dust. Not much time left. I press Argo's dead gun into the empress's smooth, slim hand. Reluctantly, she takes it. 'Keep it,' I say. 'Bring Argo home as well—if you can. He deserves that.'

For the first time since I met her, Naia seems lost for words. I smile at her.

The last thing I feel is the press of her ruby lips against my forehead.

GLAMOURWING: SACRIFICE

<u>William</u>

25th April 1915. Dawn. We are the second wave to reach the beach. The water is red with blood. Men—my brothers-in-arms—soldiers of the Australian 3rd Brigade, are falling under the machine gun fire coming from the cliffs. It's my turn to jump out of the boat. I hold my gun high. It'll jam if it gets wet. Saltwater slaps my thighs and face. The air tastes like gunpowder. All I can hear are the bullets whizzing past my head—*rat-a-tatter-tatter-tatter-tat*—and the shocked gasps of men around me as that searing lead hits them. *Join the Australian Imperial Force, William*, the government said. *Fight for your country, William*, the government said. And then, *Welcome to the Gallipoli Campaign.*

If only I knew then what I know now.

I'm lucky. I make it onto the beach without getting shot. Falling mortar shells from the artillery battery at Gabe Tepe shriek in my ears, but the cries of the dying are louder. The man to the left of me pitches sideways and doesn't get up. The back of his head is missing. The man to the right of me staggers and blood spurts from his arm, spraying out across the sand. He drops his gun but keeps running. I follow his lead. The protection of the cliffs is only fifty yards away.

The sun breaks from the east. The details of the cove grow clearer. Perpendicular crags, ridges, gullies, and gorse bushes border the beach. Hell on Earth. Another bullet whines by my ear, another mortar falls. Gravel and sand rain down over me. I grit my teeth and redouble my efforts. The cliffs are close. Others are already huddled against them, using their entrenching tools to dig for cover. I'm almost there…

But suddenly I fall.

Did I trip or was I shot?

I roll to my back, pulling my rifle free from under me. The bayonet is still fixed to the muzzle. I hold my breath waiting to see what hurts. But there's no pain. I'm okay. I did trip over some poor bloke though. He's still pressed against my back. I roll over again.

'Sorry, mate…' I begin.

But it's not a soldier.

It's a woman; a woman with emerald hair and shining, silver scales for skin.

'What the hell?' A spray of bullets kicks up the sand by my elbow. My arm flies up to protect my head. The barrage passes. I look back at the woman. She is unconscious, a lump starting to swell on her forehead. 'Jesus bloody Christ,' I mutter. I shift my rifle to my armpit and get to my feet. Huddled over, I drag the woman the last ten feet to safety.

***

Naia

The sounds of canvas flapping in the wind and quiet moans of pain waken me. I open my eyes.

Who am I?

Naia.

Where am I?

A tent.

Wounded humans dressed in green uniforms lie on stretchers around me. They stink of blood, sweat and worse. Other humans, also uniformed, fuss over them with vials, needles and white bandages.

Where am I really?

Then I remember.

I am years away from where I should be—in the past where a younger version of myself already exists. Damn the Chronohide, that foul, time travelling, fire-breathing dragon who brought me here.

I sit up. The tent lurches around me. I gasp and touch my forehead, feeling a lump there. Nausea rolls in my stomach. Everything turns hazy for a moment, then sharpens as memories flood in clamouring for attention. I left my home, the merfolk city of Amorpha, to destroy the ancient mummified body of the Chronohide dragon. I recall failing in that quest, awakening him instead when he was exposed to the naked soul of Argo—another dragon whose soul was tied to an alien-made soul gun.

And there is more.

When it all turned bad, my friend Jack Johns had faith in me. Jack, Argo's Soulslinger partner, wanted me to make things right.

Then a final memory—

I straighten, my blood thundering in my ears.

With the Chronohide having turned back time, the planet is now facing invasion.

I need to get out of here.

One of the humans realises I am awake. He makes his way past the prone bodies to me. His eyes look haunted as they connect with mine, his face grey and heavily lined. 'I'm Captain O'Brien, doctor on duty,' he says. 'You're in the Casualty Clearing Station. How's your head?'

I touch it again with a gentle finger. 'Tender, but I shall live.' The doctor glances over his shoulder, back at the rows of injured men that line the canvas tent. 'Good. That's a lot more than these other blokes can say.'

I follow his gaze. Wounds and bloodied bandages. The sight is certainly grim.

'What were you doing out there on the beach?' asks Captain O'Brien.

'I assure you it was not intentional.'

'I bloody bet it wasn't,' he replies. 'You were smack bang in the middle of the shit!'

I don't appreciate his crude bedside manner. 'Like I said, not intentional.'

'All right. I won't push it. I've got precious little time to spare as it is.' The doctor leans in. 'But one more thing about your skin. The scaling. I've never seen anything like it.' His tone turns apologetic. 'And

I'm stitched up for supplies here. I've got nothing here to ease it…'

I clutch the sheet covering my chest and pull it closer to my chin. How dare he suggest my scales are an ailment! But he does look genuinely distressed that he cannot help me. So I choose to ignore the slight. Humans of the past cannot help being ignorant. They know nothing of the truths of Eridan, the planet that in this time they call Earth. To them, merfolk and dragons are the stuff of legends.

I swallow my pride. 'Nothing to fear, Doctor. I am in no pain with it.'

Captain O'Brien seems relieved. 'I'm sorry. I really wish I could help.'

'Of course. I understand. But there is still a way you can assist me,' I say. 'If you could just tell me what year this is?'

The doctor looks at me oddly. 'Are you sure you are okay?'

'I am. It's just the exact date has escaped me.'

His brow furrows. 'It's 26th of April, 1915. You were delivered here, unconscious, along with the other wounded yesterday morning.'

April 1915. I think back to that year—a time when my father still ruled as Emperor. The ancient names and dates come slowly, but I do recall them. 'We are here fighting The Great War. Correct? And this battle is to win the Dardanelles Strait?'

The doctor reaches over and touches my head. His fingers gently prod the edge of my lump. 'Yes,' he says. Then his eyes thin, wrinkling the skin around them. He asks again. 'Why were you on the beach?'

I look up at him and smile. 'It's a long story and one I must discuss with your Commanding Officer.'

***

William

Captain O'Brien figured as I was the one to find the woman, I should be the one to take her to see the Major General. She's been given a uniform to wear, which is good, as she was distracting dressed in only those strange scales of hers. I lead her out the hospital tent and head towards the Officer's digs. Soldiers gathered in small groups, smoking, watch us as we pass. Whispers follow in our wake. The story of the woman on the beach has spread, it seems.

There is no avoiding the makeshift morgue pegged out by the side of the Clearing Station. The woman trails me closely as we pass the bodies. Even with the bloodstained sheets covering them, lax hands and the odd foot have worked their way clear. The brutal nature of their deaths cannot be hidden. I glance at the woman. Her face is set like stone, her gaze trained forward. She moves unfazed, as if the truth of warfare is not unfamiliar to her.

I've never met a woman so tough before.

Major General Bridges' tent is just ahead. I recognise the guard by the door. 'Here to see the Boss, Jimmy,' I say to him.

He nods and tips his chin towards the tent flap. 'Just inside, mate.'

The Major General is at his desk, leaning over a map. I recognise the outline of the Dardanelles Strait spidering across the yellow paper. He looks up, his pale blue eyes like chips of ice. 'Private, what is it?'

I salute. 'The woman Captain O'Brien messaged you about, Sir.'

Bridges pushes himself upright. His lips are a tight line below his neatly trimmed moustache. 'Yes. The woman.' His gaze shifts to her. 'What in God's name where you doing out there? From what I hear, you would be dead if it wasn't for Private Johns here.'

I've seen grown men shrink beneath the Major General's stare, but not this woman. She scrutinises him for a moment, as if to challenge him, then slowly turns. Her green eyes take in everything about me. I resist the urge to squirm.

'Is that true, soldier? You pulled me from the beach?'

I glance at Bridges before answering. 'Yes ma'am. And also gave you the bump on your head. Sorry about that.'

The woman's fingers flinch as if recalling the accidental blow. 'No. The fault was mine. I thank you for your bravery.' She turns back to the Major General. 'You are the Commanding Officer here?'

'Yes. Major General Bridges of the 1st Division.'

'Good. I am Empress Naia of the Merfolk. I need your help.' The way she says it, it's as if she has every right in the world to ask him for anything. 'There is an attack imminent on our planet,' she says. 'We are threatened by beings from the stars—aliens named the Tinkervaatch. I am in a unique position to defend against them, but not alone. I will need a company of your men. You can continue to defend the beaches, and I will take them to the hills to locate and ward off the new threat.'

Bridges frowns. His hair catches the sunlight from the window, tinting it silver. 'Empress Naia, is it?' he says.

'Yes.'

'Let me get this straight. You want me to give you men to take up into the occupied hills?'

'That is correct.'

'To defend against these…aliens?'

'Yes.'

My superior's smile holds no warmth. 'Look lady,' he says. 'I don't know where you have come from, but I don't have time for this. I've got Turks breathing down my neck, and the brass won't let me evacuate my men.' He looks at me. 'Private. Escort the lady to the beach. Put her on one of the boats heading out with the wounded. She'll be safer on the ships than here.'

'Yes, sir.' I turn to take the woman by the arm, but she is faster than me. She steps forward out of my grasp and glares up into Bridges' face.

This woman is no stranger to commanding men.

'What are you afraid of, Major General? That I will kill your soldiers?' says Naia. She points to the door. 'They are already out there dying. At least let them have a chance to do so defending their planet.' Her hand drops to her side. 'Believe me when I say your fight will end here. Your men will never gain the Strait. They will perish on these very cliffs you cling to. Do not waste their loyalty. Give them a task worthy of their mettle. Let them help me. Do so, or see us all enslaved.'

The Major General is tough. He doesn't back down. 'Private,' he repeats carefully, as if holding his temper in check. 'Take her to the boats.'

Naia holds nothing back. She slams a hand down on the desk. The maps jump. 'I will not go,' she says.

Bridges' mouth flattens to a grim line. 'Go, or you will be arrested.'

'Try it and see what happens.'

Something about her determination inspires me. Maybe it's that she reminds me of the soldier I saw on the beach—the man who was wounded, lost his gun but kept running. 'Sir,' I say before I think. 'Maybe we can't spare a whole company, but with your permission, I'll escort her where she wants to go.'

Bridges' gaze snaps to me. He isn't the kind of man to stand down from a fight. But he's also busy and wants the woman gone. 'I'll take her, and when we find nothing,' I say, 'I'll return her to the boats as you've ordered.'

The Major General considers my proposal then nods. 'Be back in two days,' he says. 'Now get her out of my sight.'

***

Naia

One man is better than none. Private Johns seems young, but on closer inspection, he looks capable. His steps are sure as he leads me up the ravine to the plateau the Allied troops secured the previous day. Plugge's Plateau. The climb is brutal, with the bushes coarse against my hands and the stones crumbling away beneath my feet.

I believe the aliens will be holed up in the hills away from the fighting. It is their most likely course of action. They will need to regroup, prepare to fight the humans for supremacy of the planet, and work out how to locate what they have come to hunt—the hidden dragons of this age.

Lucky for me, I already know where to find them.

Private Johns mentioned seeing a small cave, located in an adjoining gully, visible from the top of the plateau.

A cave means dragons, and dragons will be allies.

When we crest the ridge, the view past the plateau is breathtaking—hills, endless sea and blue skies. But the small, flat table of land itself is massacred. A mess of abandoned trenches and tumbled coils of barbed wire litter the top. The boy does not seem surprised by the ugliness of it all. Instead he stands for a moment to catch his breath, rifle placed upright for support.

I too am thankful for the short reprieve.

Finally, he raises his hand, pointing down the left-hand side of the plateau. A small, rugged gully, edged with trees, presses in close to the base of the hill. 'There it is. The cave.'

The entrance is not obvious unless you know where to look. Being shown, it's easy to see the irregular hole carved into the sand-coloured cliffs and the battered bushes on the faint path leading to it. 'Perfect,' I say. 'Ready to head down?'

The boy smiles, 'Ready as I'll ever be, ma'am.'

I look at him. 'Your name is William isn't it?'

'Yeah.'

'You may call me Naia.'

'Naia, then,' he says, shouldering his rifle.

***

The edges of the cave opening are scratched and scored. The ground is soft, powdered sand. William remains at my back as I investigate, his rifle ready and gaze pinned to the rugged hills. Even under his people's control, this land is dangerous. I am glad for his dedication to his soldier duties.

The acrid smell of a dragon's breath is strong in the air. This cave is most certainly a den. My boot shifts the loose sand. A glittering spark of light catches my attention. I lean in. An opal-coloured scale. I press my fingertip to it. It sticks. 'We are in luck, William.'

'What is it?'

'A dragon's scale,' I reply.

William leans over to look. 'That's a lizard's scale.'

'No. It's dragon.'

William looks at me like I am crazy. 'Dragons don't exist,' he says.

I smile. 'Next you will be telling me that mermaids don't either.'

William's brow furrows. 'They don't.'

***

William

I grew out of believing in fairy tales a long time ago. Dragons are not real. There must be some other explanation for the scale and the turpentine smell coming from the hole. But there is no time to dwell on it. Standing out in the open makes me nervous.

'Are we going in to take a look?' I ask.

Naia seems hesitant. 'Dragons in this age are much less civilised than in my time. We must proceed cautiously.'

I don't need another conversation on the reality of dragons. So I humour her. 'What are we going to do then?'

'Wait for the dragon to come to us.'

'It's too dangerous out here, Naia.'

A stone suddenly explodes three feet from my head, followed by the sound of a gunshot. The delay between the impact and the sound tells me everything I need to know.

Sniper.

'What was that?' gasps Naia.

I drag her down, making us smaller targets. 'Trouble. We need to get inside.'

Another shattered stone. Another gunshot. I wrench Naia towards the cave.

But we don't make it.

Thrown to the ground by a sudden blast of wind, I cast an arm across Naia to protect her. I squint through a curtain of dust.

And I see something.

An invisible *force*.

The edge of the transparent shape catches the top of the cave's mouth as it exits. Its invisibility splinters to reveal a momentary flash of multi-hued scales and long, wicked, blue spikes. Then the shape is gone, invisible again, as it launches into the sky.

Naia claps a hand on my shoulder and laughs. 'See!' she says. 'A glamoured dragon! I told you they are real. Now watch!'

And I do. I follow the flight of the shape, watching it climb as clouds and escarpments distort behind it. It sheers to the left, ascending along the edge of the ravine. Then it banks sharply and halts to hover in front of a far cliff. A cloud of something grey appears out of nowhere, billowing out to consume the stone. Then the bluff explodes. Within the falling rubble, the enemy sniper somersaults, his rifle pin-wheeling behind him.

Naia cheers, her fist punching the air. 'It's a Glamourwing!' she says excitedly. 'They can render themselves invisible and their breath is gaseous. Deadly when inhaled, and highly explosive.'

Speechless, I watch as the huge, transparent blur swings back around and lands ten feet away from us.

Through another cloud of dust, a deep, disembodied voice rumbles out. 'Well met, Empress Naia.'

Naia's exuberance fades. She stands stock-still. 'Can it be?' she whispers. Then louder, 'Sheerwing?'

The air seems to shiver, and the blur drops away like a curtain. The details of a huge reptile are revealed. His glittering body, coloured like a peacock's, is every imaginable shade of green, blue, red and gold. Sapphire spikes collar his neck and run down the length of his spine. His deep, violet-coloured eyes are full of ancient wisdom.

I suck in a breath.

And for the first time since I was a child, I believe in dragons.

***

In my time, Sheerwing, one of the greatest allies of my people, is dead. He sacrificed himself to imprison a deadly mage and in doing so, paved the way for peace between humans and dragons. It has been many years since I last saw him. I find myself holding back tears as I place my hand on his long elegant snout.

'Well met indeed, dear friend.'

'You are a vision of loveliness, my dear,' says the dragon.

Glamourwings. Always the charmers! 'And as always, Sheerwing,' I reply, 'you are much too kind to me.'

William shuffles behind me. I turn. 'Step forward, soldier. Meet one of the greatest drakes of your time.' I point. 'Sheerwing.'

'But…'

Sheerwing smiles at the boy with a silver-toothed grin. 'I was listening earlier. You don't believe in dragons?' he says.

'I don't know what the hell to believe anymore,' says William.

'Well, if nothing else, believe this. You have no need to fear me, human,' says the Glamourwing. 'A friend of Empress Naia is a friend of mine.'

***

Glamourwings, although deadly, are omnivorous pacifists that covet beauty. As such, Sheerwing's den is well appointed with edible food and is stunning in its décor. Only the strange smell of his breath marks the place as belonging to a saurian.

A small fire crackles merrily in a low, stone-lined pit. The light illuminates the den and reflects off the dragon hoard that lines the shelved walls. Gold vases, fine ceramics, and brilliant-cut gems. William sits stiffly next to me, his rifle laid across his knees. I suppose I cannot blame him for his unease. Life, before today, was much simpler for him to understand.

Having just finished explaining to Sheerwing the details of my quest and imparting the importance of its success, I lean back against a tapestried floor cushion and select an apple from a low, polished granite bowl. The flesh is sweet when I bite into it.

Sheerwing, curled around the fire with eyes half lidded, considers my words. 'I have seen those for whom you search,' he says. 'For the last two months, a non-human force has been gathering in a concealed area to the east. I have been monitoring them. They seem to be preparing for something—building complex machines and amassing an arsenal of advanced weaponry.'

Two months? The timeline shift must have landed the Tinkervaatch here earlier than myself. A concerning state of affairs. They will have had time to prepare. I lean forward. 'What type of weapons?'

'Several kinds. Mostly hand-held firearms,' says the dragon. 'But they are unsettling. The guns glow with strange lights and are made of metal that whispers.' Sheerwing shudders as if shaking off ghosts. 'There is also something more.'

'Yes?'

'The fire-breathing dragon you seek. They have captured him.'

I suck in a breath. 'You're sure? The fire-breather is imprisoned?'

'Yes,' says Sheerwing. 'But he does not look to be well cared for. I have been considering a sortie to liberate him.'

'Good Goddess of the Sea, Sheerwing,' I say. 'That beast is the Chronohide. Primal and brutal. We can't release him. We need to stop him!'

'He does not look so savage,' says Sheerwing.

'Do not doubt me. He is a primordial beast. If allowed to, he will travel through time until he has consumed everything. We cannot let him endure.'

Sheerwing sighs. 'I do not enjoy destroying my brethren, Naia. Even for a good cause.'

'I regret the necessity also.'

'How then do you propose to kill him?'

'We cannot kill him.' I look down. 'The best we can hope for is to bind him. The Trinity of Creation will do it—a mix of human, dragon and merfolk blood applied to his hide. We just need to get close enough to do it.'

Sheerwing looks up, his violet eyes glittering. 'If it must be done, then you have my support. And what of those who have imprisoned him?'

I frown. 'The Tinkervaatch cannot be allowed to enslave any more dragons. They must be dealt with. You are our greatest weapon in that regard.'

Sheerwing nods, his long elegant head catching the light and flicking green and blue glints over my skin. 'So the mission is set. The binding of our brother, the Chronohide, and death to the invaders.' His gaze flicks across to William. 'Will you be joining us in our quest, young man?'

William blinks. 'I've got your back, Sir.'

'I am glad for it,' replies Sheerwing. 'And speaking of backs, I trust you know how to hold on to one?'

***

William

Holy bloody hell. It's terrifying flying through the air, clinging to the back of a dragon. The wind roars by my ears and the scales are as slippery as oil. Holding on to Naia's waist, and hoping, are all I can do to avoid a fall to death.

But even with the fear, I can't deny the view is beautiful. From up here, the hospital ships are visible at anchor, dotted off the coast. I see the twinkle of guns firing on the ridges and the ant-like figures of soldiers fighting to gain ground. It's interesting how without the immediacy of the gunfire, the screams and the gore, war doesn't look so brutal.

It's not long before we reach our objective. Sheerwing, concealing us within his glamour, climbs higher, then falls into a circling pattern above a valley surrounded by thick scrubland. And the scene is just as he said—a clearing full of gleaming gold machines, racks of strange-looking weapons, and two-legged people that look nothing like humans.

And a cage holding a blood-red dragon.

A dragon at least five times the size of Sheerwing.

The creature's bulk has been of no use to him. He looks worn thin, as if he has fought hard but failed to secure his freedom. A part of me can't help but feel sorry for the animal.

Naia shifts. She leans over Sheerwing's neck. 'Take us in closer,' she says to him.

Sheerwing banks to the left and loses height. Still invisible, he lands us quietly at the edge of the clearing. The Tinkervaatch move oblivious amongst the machines. Their long, white hair, thin bodies, pale faces and glowing red eyes mark them as very different to humans. They look cold and brutal. Cruel. I shudder. I prefer taking on the Turks; at least they are an enemy I understand.

Naia's disembodied whisper catches my ear. 'We need to get closer to the Chronohide. Can you get us there, Sheerwing?'

I sense the dragon's nod—a slight pulse of displaced air. 'Yes. Hold my shoulder. I will lead you.'

The Chronohide's cage is in the centre of the clearing surrounded by racks of guns. Sheerwing, leads us through them, choosing routes less trafficked. As the weapons file by, I observe sparks dancing in the clear cylinders fixed above the barrels. Strange lights—lights that set my neck hairs prickling.

Finally, the cage looms large in the growing dusk. The Chronohide's huge bulk is slumped on the floor. Dry blood stains his shoulders, leaking from wounds almost hidden by the darkness of his hide. He shifts minutely, as if to ease the pain of cramped muscles. The edges of his wings flare suddenly with fire then die down again to embers.

The dragon in the cage shifts again. This time he sniffs the air, his nostrils flaring. 'I smell you, brother,' he whispers. 'A Glamourwing, are you not?

And you have others with you. Please come closer. You have nothing to fear from me.' Then the dragon opens his eyes, a clear, pure silver colour against the rough bulk of his rugged hide.

'Do not trust him, Sheerwing,' hisses Naia. 'He is dangerous.'

The scarlet dragon chuckles, a lonely sound. 'You fear the Chronohide. Yet I am not he. But do as you see fit. End this. I grow weary of being a slave to the Tinkervaatch.'

Naia hesitates. 'If you are not the Chronohide,' she says, 'then who are you?'

The dragon raises his head, higher this time. 'My name is Argo. I am neither a time-bender nor immortal. I have no access to the powers of the Chronohide. I have only taken control of his body by binding his mind with my own. But if you require additional proof, here it is—I recognise you, merwoman. I have visited your halls. You are the Empress Naia of Amorpha.'

I hear Naia's sharp intake of breath.

She doesn't say another word.

***

Argo? Can it really be? I take a step towards the wretched creature and peer into its startling silver eyes. A vision comes back to me of the future—my future in which the Chronohide consumed Argo's soul, a future when the Chronohide's eyes were coloured green.

Shattershrew dragons have silver eyes.

Argo was a Shattershrew.

'If you are truly Argo, then name your Soulslinger.'

The Chronohide drops his head back to the base of his cage. 'Jack Johns. And what I would not give to have him here.'

The face of the Soulslinger I knew in my own time flits before my eyes. The last words he spoke float back to me... *Bring Argo home as well. If you can. He deserves that.*

'Get him out of the cage,' I whisper.

'Excuse me?' asks Sheerwing.

'I said, get him out.'

William's invisible shoulder brushes against mine. 'Let me try,' he says.

A quiet clank of steel against steel. The lock on Argo's cage shivers. The boy must be using his bayonet to lever against it.

There is a quiet grunt of exertion and the sound of metal snapping. The broken end of a knife materialises just before it falls into the dust by the cage. 'Dammit,' curses William. 'Broke it!'

'Let me try.' I pick up the end of the broken blade and tease the tip of it into the lock. I twist it expertly and the lock springs open. I catch it in my hand.

'Years spent opening oysters?' whispers Sheerwing.

'An underestimated skill,' I reply, smiling.

The door to Argo's cage swings open on silent hinges. He shuffles forward, his claws scraping at the metal floor, his wings pushing him outward.

In moments he is clear.

But then I hear a cry.

'The dragon is free! Guards, to me!'

The Tinkervaatch. They have discovered us.

***

William

Sheerwing's glamour drops as soon as the Tinkervaatch start filing in past the racks of weapons. Now visible also, I huddle in close to Naia. In the growing darkness, the aliens look like demons with their red eyes glowing. They all carry golden guns in their hands, each one loaded with a spark of light.

And those sparks whisper to me.

'Soul guns!' cries Argo. 'We cannot win. Flee!'

But it's too late to run. And I am trained to fight for my life. I jab my rifle to my shoulder, aim and fire.

The first Tinkervaatch slumps over, his gun skittering into the dirt. I slide the bolt and eject the cartridge. Another gunshot, another one falls dead. A buzzing sound starts next my left ear. I turn, clearing the rifle bolt again as I go. Another alien bears down on me. I shoot. That Tinkervaatch drops and the light of his weapon fades.

Argo calls out, but this time, to Sheerwing. 'Together, brother!'

I fall back, pulling Naia with me. Her fingernails dig into my shoulder as we watch the two drakes advance. Side by side—the Chronohide and the Glamourwing. Their eyes flash, their wings extend high—my heart swells at their power and majesty.

Argo's wings flare wider, their edges erupting with fire. He roars and a torrent of flame bursts from his jaws and consumes the closest group of Tinkervaatch. Their cries rise up as their bodies, clothed in flame, twist and turn before falling to the ground. The gun racks catch alight also.

Sheerwing follows Argo's lead. He is smaller but his breath is twice as deadly. Silhouetted against

Argo's fire, he opens his mouth and launches a billowing stream of grey gas into the flames.

An explosion rocks the clearing.

More Tinkervaatch fall.

But it isn't enough.

Additional aliens pour into the clearing. With them come several shots from soul guns. Balls of light, gold, green and silver erupt into the dusk, shifting their shape as they fly to resemble dragons.

Dragon souls.

As one, they all turn, headed for Argo and Sheerwing.

The first blast hits Argo's chest. He stumbles backward, his rear legs giving way beneath him. Another hits him on the side. He screams. I step forward, but Naia pulls me back. 'The dragons' hides protect them, but we are powerless against weapons like those!'

Frustrated, I look back. The third soul careens towards Sheerwing. It hits him in the side of the skull and flings him across the clearing. He lands hard, purple blood spraying from his nostrils.

Down but not broken, Sheerwing lumbers back to his feet. With a thrust of his wings, he jumps and is airborne. He crosses the clearing, scattering the souls that circle Argo. 'Up!' screams the Glamourwing at the prone dragon. 'Get up and fight!'

But Argo is done. Weakened with exhaustion, he tries to rise but collapses again to the ground, unconscious.

Sheerwing's roar of frustration is laced with his gaseous breath. The scent of it rolls over me a like a wave. The smaller dragon hovers for a moment as if uncertain what to do.

The aliens advance.

More soul shots are fired. The scene is lit up like Christmas.

I catch and hold Sheerwing's violet gaze. I can't tell what he's thinking. But Naia can.

'NO,' screams the empress. 'THERE MUST BE ANOTHER WAY!'

Sheerwing turns.

In that moment, I am transfixed. Argo lies on the ground, unconscious and bleeding. Naia is screaming by my ear. The sounds of gunfire and the dying fill the air. But Sheerwing's grace transcends it all. He climbs higher into the sky, a glittering opal butterfly.

The lines of his body begin to shine. From the tip of his tail to the lengths of his long, silver teeth, a blue-white light encircles him. Lightning flashes down from the clear sky overhead, drawn and captured by his body. His form starts to grow, larger and larger until he outsizes the clearing. The Tinkervaatch stop firing. Their pale faces, illuminated by Sheerwing's light, lift to the sky.

Then everything grows silent. Time seems to slow. All that exists is the great, glowing drake and those of us who stand beneath him.

Thunder rolls, and in a final, blinding clap of lightning, Sheerwing arches his neck. His chest peels open, and revealed is his core—not flesh and blood, but a ball of spinning, multicoloured light. As the glow expands, his heart becomes a doorway to a garden I can only just glimpse past the veil of brightness. Then Sheerwing crumples—the butterfly broken. He falls to the ground dead, his wings and body encompassing all.

***

Naia

Sheerwing's magic rushes over my skin like the rising tide. It is soft and gentle; beautiful like all the things he loved in life. I want to scream out my anguish but find I am voiceless in the cradle of his power.

My friend has sacrificed himself to save us. Drawing on his birthright, the blood magic that belongs to all Glamourwings, he opened a portal and behind it created a new dimension—a dimension beyond time and space neatly contained within the boundary of his bones.

A place in which the Tinkervaatch are now imprisoned.

Somehow, Sheerwing has held us separate. We ride on currents of air and light, our travel smooth and safe. I am aware of William somewhere close beside me and can sense the vibrations of Argo's rumbling breaths. I do not know where we are being taken, so resign myself to waiting.

I sense the approach of others—the dragons that were trapped in the soul guns. Now free, they exist as motes of light dancing in the flux of magic. They rush by me, a helter-skelter river of life, headed for some other destination. Their joy in freedom is palpable.

***

How long has it been since our battle with the Tinkervaatch? Seconds or days? I cannot tell. All I know is that when I wake, Argo and William slumber alongside me. We are concealed in the shrubby trees that line the edge of Sheerwing's ravine. His cave hunkers nearby in the dawn's light. I stand up and brush the dust off my pants. Argo is sleeping fitfully, with no sign of any wounds, but William is awake. He groans as he rolls over. Sitting up, he instinctively reaches for the rifle lying by his side.

'Where are we?' He rubs at his eyes.

'Sheerwing somehow sent us back,' I say.

William looks around. 'What happened to him?' he asks.

I turn my gaze to the sky, my heart heavy. 'He imprisoned the Tinkervaatch to save us. He sacrificed his own life to do so.'

William rubs the back of his hand under his nose. 'I don't know about your kind or what happens in your time, Naia,' he says. 'But here, we honour our fallen brothers by remembering them. I won't forget what he did for us.'

'I shall not either,' I say, dropping my gaze to meet his. 'His memory will live on in us.'

William smiles, albeit sadly. 'So, you've done what you came to do. What happens now?'

And I find I do not know. Argo cannot take us home, and I cannot return to my people. They already have a version of me waiting to take the throne when their Emperor dies. I cannot let my existence in this time muddy that succession. I sigh. 'While I prefer the ocean to land,' I say, 'I think my fate is to remain here.' I point over my shoulder. 'Sheerwing's den is comfortable.'

'But it's in the middle of a warzone,' says William.

'I have Argo to protect me. And you, if you choose to stay.'

William looks shocked. 'Stay?' he says. 'I'm sorry, Naia. But I have to get back. Can't leave the blokes to fight this war alone.' A cheeky grin crosses his lips. 'And if I'm down there, I can try and make sure we keep this ground. You know, help keep you both safe.'

If my time with William has shown me one thing, it is that he is loyal to a fault. I knew he wouldn't stay. I ask one final question. 'What will you do when your war is over?'

William looks up to the ridge that rises above us. I follow the line of his gaze. Even this far away, the barbed wire and trenches are visible bristling on the crest. 'If I'm lucky enough to make it out alive,' he says, 'I think I'll head for America.' He looks back at me. 'I always wanted to see the Wild West. You know, learn about cowboys and Indians, gunslingers and such.'

'Then that is what I will hope for you, William.'

The boy smiles and tips two fingers to his forehead in a casual salute. 'Well then, Empress Naia. If my services are no longer needed. I'll be heading back.'

I smile. 'Of course.'

He turns to go, but then pauses. 'Thanks for everything, and I do mean everything.' He glances across at the sleeping bulk of Argo. 'It's nice to know that some myths are real.'

I walk to him and enfold him in my arms. He embraces me back awkwardly. 'My thanks to you also, brave soldier. It is comforting to know that not all humans in this time are ignorant of the truth.'

William steps back. 'Goodbye, Naia.'

'Goodbye, William.'

As the boy walks away, I am struck by how childlike his frame looks against the length of his rifle. I find myself hoping he will live through the turmoil of the war, and that he will make it to America—the place known as the Western Reach in my time. Argo, now awake, moves to stand beside me. His gaze follows William's receding form. The weight of his sadness hangs over him.

'Argo?'

His silver eyes turn to me. 'I am sorry, Empress. Sorry I could not protect Sheerwing. Sorry I cannot take us home. This is not the ending I hoped for.'

'Do not be so hard on yourself. I have no regrets.'

'But we are out of our time. We have no life here.'

I sigh. 'Argo, back home I am Empress of Amorpha. But I also have another name. Sacrifice. For it is my duty to give up all I have, including my life, should it be required. I do not resent my fate, but instead see it as a culmination of my responsibility to my people.'

'How so?'

'Can you not see it?' I ask. 'We may be trapped here, but we have succeeded. Our sacrifice has saved those we love. The Tinkervaatch are imprisoned, and the Chronohide is contained. No threat remains.'

'That is true,' says the dragon. 'But I would have liked to see home again. Just once.'

'We are both long-lived,' I reply. 'So you will, in time. But until then we have work to do. By saving us here, Sheerwing can no longer save our world in the future. We need to fill that breach.'

'So you mean it's up to us to stop invasion by evil mages, oversee the forging of peace accords between dragons and humans and curb the greed of sky dragons?'

'We can only try.'

Argo grows serious. 'And what of Jack? Do you think I shall ever see him again?'

'I am certain of it.'

Argo's gaze grows distant. 'So what about right now? What are we to do?'

I place a hand on Argo's broad shoulder. The heat of his fiery blood rises off his hide. 'There is only one thing we can do, my friend. We take a moment—a moment to remember our fallen and give thanks for their sacrifice.'

About the Author

Pamela Jeffs is a speculative-fiction author living in Queensland, Australia with her husband and two daughters. Her work has been published previously in various magazines and anthologies and has been twice nominated for Australian Aurealis Awards.

Prior to pursuing her passion for writing, Pamela's background was in interior and exhibition design. This allowed her to collaborate with a multitude of talented artists and designers across a number of artistic platforms.

Five Dragons is her third collection.

To discover more books by Pamela Jeffs and be notified of new releases, deals and specials, visit and subscribe at:

www.pamelajeffs.com
Twitter: @Pamela_Jeffs
Facebook: @pamelajeffsauthor

OTHER TITLES

Discover other titles by Pamela Jeffs at:
www.pamelajeffs.com

Including:

Red Hour and Other Strange Tales
Saloons & Stardust: A Collection
Turtle Island

If you enjoyed this book, please go to Goodreads
and/or Amazon and leave a review. It helps
Thank you.